P

Edi

Barry used to watch the Bute Street Site from his window every school day, waiting for the children to come and the Game to begin – waiting, above all, for one special girl. Fascinated by her graceful energy, he called her 'the Indian Queen', but he'd never met her and could only guess what she was really like. Then came a day when, desperate to warn his unknown friend that she was in danger, Barry threw a flowerpot – and she looked up and saw him.

West Indian Hal lived in a block of high-rise flats with nowhere to play for miles around, so it was a godsend when she discovered a way into the derelict site, a jungle where she and her friends could do as they liked. Once she'd found out about Barry, how he lived alone with his mother, was just getting over a long illness, and was terrified of going outside the house, she decided to make life more interesting for him. True, he *was* a bit of a creep, the way he was so helpless and clinging, but he was on her mind now. And she *did* help him. She got him out on to the site where, playing with the other kids and helping to set up the new adventure playground, he grew more buoyant by the day and at last found the courage to return to school. In fact, Hal was to find herself amazed at just how tough and resourceful Barry could be.

Full of the vitality of the rough London street life it describes, this fine novel is, too, a sensitive account of how a friendship grows between two teenagers. For readers of twelve and over.

Jean MacGibbon

HAL

PUFFIN BOOKS

Puffin Books, Penguin Books Ltd, Harmondsworth, Middlesex, England
Penguin Books, 625 Madison Avenue, New York, New York 10022, U.S.A.
Penguin Books Australia Ltd, Ringwood, Victoria, Australia
Penguin Books Canada Ltd, 2801 John Street, Markham, Ontario, Canada L3R 1B4
Penguin Books (N.Z.) Ltd, 182–190 Wairau Road, Auckland 10, New Zealand

—

First published by William Heinemann Ltd 1974
Published in Puffin Books 1978

—

—

Made and printed in Great Britain by
C. Nicholls & Company Ltd
Set in Linotype Juliana

To James

One

FROM the back window at the top of a tall house a boy looked out. His whole body was tense, crouched on a box to give him height, his thin arms in his new jersey pressed down on the dirty sill.

He was waiting for the children to come. Ever since he and his mother had moved from the place where they had lived before, after he was well enough to leave hospital, Barry Padgitt had spent every weekday here up in this high room while his mother was out at work. He had been afraid to go out alone since his illness; though sometimes in the evenings and at weekends she took him out.

Every school day he watched the clock, waiting for the children to come. Waiting for the Game to begin. Waiting, above all, for one special girl.

He was looking beyond the narrow back gardens of the terrace where he lived down on to a wide expanse of ground, which in the midst of a great, crowded city, had been left to grow wild. The Bute Street Site was unsafe for building on because of a network of railway tunnels below, and didn't seem to be useful for anything else. Its miniature small-scale hills and valleys, mostly covered with dense undergrowth and clumps of young trees, made an ideal place for all kinds of games, or, if you were too old for games, Barry thought, just a super place to lie around in. There was one particular hill crowned with three saplings where he longed to stretch out; but so great was his fear of leaving his room that the idea seemed dream-like.

Meanwhile there were the children to watch and wait for. The site was bounded on two sides by houses, the further terrace almost hidden by light summer foliage. There was a secret, private air about the place, an expectant, watchful stillness. Away to the right there towered a large, castle-like building, the Bute Institute. To his left the site was bounded by a high wall beyond which, had he ever been out to look, he would have found the canal.

It was between this wall and the end garden of his terrace that the girl and her friends had found a narrow gap; and when school was over they would squeeze through, stealthily, in twos and threes, careful not to be told off for trespassing, though once inside they soon forgot.

The tall girl came first, and the very sight of her made his heart beat painfully on the hard ledge. She was Barry's age, or perhaps a bit younger, brown-skinned, her bare legs very long, her black hair tied up with a scarlet ribbon. Her hands held the hands of two very small girls, their hair done up in intricate plaits, followed by two older girls and two boys, one carrying a shopping bag with a bottle sticking out of it. Others joined the little group; but it was the tall girl Barry cared about. He knew what she would do next: she pushed the two little girls before her into the bushes, took the bag and disappeared after them, bending double under the interlaced branches.

She was putting them in a safe place before the battle began. These bushes were riddled with narrow paths like tunnels. The bushes trembled and eddied like water when a fish darts about just under the surface, and Barry could trace her serpentine course which brought the three to a central hiding-place, some prickly green cavern.

He watched for the girl to re-emerge – there she was! The waiting girls and boys pressed round her. She was their leader; that was clear. She disposed of her troops; they disappeared in the scrub. All this time Barry kept an eye on the whole battlefield – for that was how he thought of it, two 'kingdoms' separated by a wide grassy strip; territories fought for but never won, trophies seized and prisoners held. Barry never worked out what the rules were, and it wasn't important for him to know. He had his own ideas about what he saw, and to know too much might have spoiled them for him. In his mind the girl was 'The Indian Queen' (the name of a pub where he and his mum had once lived). Her treasure, Indian gold, was buried where it would never be found till she herself was captured, and this had never happened yet.

By now the enemy was gathered together at the opposite end of the battlefield. They had made their stealthy entry through the Institute grounds. Barry had soon learnt to pick out their leader, 'the Spaniard', as he called him. He wore steel-rimmed glasses and an old bush hat with a cocked brim, and when it fell off his dark hair stood up in tufts. He wasn't the tallest of his gang, though thick-set and broad-shouldered, and Barry couldn't see why the others let him boss them about, except that he could whistle, piercingly and commandingly, through his teeth; also from time to time he shinned up a difficult tree near his headquarters, a feat which no one else attempted.

Today, as every day, a war had begun, a guerrilla war of stalking, concealment and surprise. The whole battlefield seemed to be in movement, bushes tossed in waves whose direction only Barry could see. Contestants crossed and re-crossed the open grassy space opposite his window which was neutral territory, 'No-man's land,' as Barry thought of it. This grassy space surrounded a low brick air-vent like a wide chimney that must have once belched smoke as trains thundered and shook below. Now that there were no steam trains it was like an extinct volcano.

Barry watched a boy and a girl dodging round it. She was quick on her feet, and the clumsier boy lunged, grabbed and lost her. At last he got her down. They rolled this way and that and it was obvious to Barry that the boy could have rolled his captive away from her base towards his own easily enough if he had really wanted to end the struggle. It was half a game, half a fight they were enjoying. Once captured and taken into the 'jungle' on either side no prisoner returned to the open.

The game must have meant more than it appeared to, Barry reckoned; for many of the boys and girls – including his favourite girl – were too old to be playing it. In spite of his vantage point, Barry could only see part of what went on, and this increased his curiosity and tension.

What he longed for was a sight of the Indian Queen; but she did not show herself often. In the jungle she was everywhere, or so he imagined, in every wave that shook the bushes, luring invaders along the tortuous tunnels, tricking them, lying in wait.

Some of this Barry saw, some invented as he crouched on his padded box trembling, clinging to the hot sill. Still weakened by his illness, to look at anything for too long tired him. And these children, this game – he was not so much *looking* at them as being them; when they were not there he felt empty, dead inside. But being too much with them was more than he could bear.

If only the Indian Queen would appear ... And there, where he would least have expected her, she was! Wriggling on her belly towards a shallow ditch that ran parallel to the garden wall of Barry's terrace, a ditch which continued round the back of the Spaniard's territory.

But the Spaniard chose this moment to shin up his tree. He spied the girl and slid down, licking through the bushes towards her. Barry guessed he meant to lie in wait and take her prisoner. How could she be warned?

Barry seized a flowerpot from the sill and hurled it with all his scant strength. The girl looked up, saw Barry's warning gesture, and ran for cover.

The Spaniard reached her just before she crossed her own boundary. He grabbed her round the neck, she tripped him, and they fell. This way and that they fought, almost on the line.

Now the jungle was full of heads; the Indians waited. Because they were so near the line the Spaniard's strength was little use to him. When he tried to roll away, the girl clung to him, choked him like a jungle creeper. His response was to roll on top of her; he put his hands on her throat and the girl went limp.

Uncertainly the Spaniard sat up astride her. Too quick for Barry to see she wriggled off balance, cast herself over her own boundary and he fell with her. The Indian Queen had won!

The game was over. Barry had wanted her to win. At least, he hadn't wanted her to lose ... He turned his back to the window. He had wanted the fight to go on and on, with neither side victorious, he hadn't foreseen the possibility of what had just happened.

He turned his back on the bright day, the late afternoon sunshine thickening over the battlefield, now stilled. The little room, by contrast, was dark. Everything in it seemed strange because his head was full of the brightness outside, the waving bushes, the boys and girls falling over each other.

Two

HAL Piercy awoke as usual to hear her two small sisters, Anda and Bell, squabbling and chattering in the bed they shared next to hers. She had been dreaming about a face high up in a window. A child who couldn't get out. She'd been trying desperately, in her dream, to find a way in, to get to the child. She woke sweating.

Neighbours on three sides of their flat had the radio going full out, and above her head hurrying footsteps confirmed what she knew already – that she was going to be late for school. Rain beat on the window, and round the window-frame a stain was spreading. The Piercy flat was on the seventh floor of a tower block and when the wind blew from the west nothing would stop rain driving in; and though Hal's father, an inventive man, had suggested to the Council that the windows could be weatherproofed like those of a bus, nothing had come of the idea.

'Get up – quick!' Hal pushed back her bed-clothes and stumbled, as though drugged, over to the window. For the past six weeks, almost every morning had been fine. Hal shivered slightly in her short nightdress, watching rain drifting over the immense open view of railway lines criss-crossing and curving away towards the distant pinnacles of the terminus, of mazey little streets dominated by factories and chimneys and tall blocks sticking up like rocks in a grey ocean.

There'd be no going to the site today, unless the weather cleared up. The thought was almost a relief. Hal had begun to be a bit bored by the Bute Street Site, marvellous though it had been when she first discovered this wild, secret place surrounded by houses. Trouble was, it was no longer 'secret'. Too many others had found their way in.

Turning back to the room she groped for her sisters' pants under the bed, flung their dresses at them and dived into her own green-checked school gingham. Their hair would have to stay as it was, done up in tiny, intricate plaits tied with red bows. Her father had come from the West Indies, and though he had lived almost all his life in England, still insisted on the two youngest girls having their hair plaited. And it was Hal's job to see to it! She herself had defied her Dad as soon as she was old enough and wore hers short.

In the kitchen her brother Benjie was shovelling down the last of his cornflakes. Cereal, sugar and milk had been left ready on the table before their mother went out to work at six a.m.

'You're late,' he said.

'Couldn't you've given me a shout?' She dumped the two kids into chairs, shook out the last of the packet, and stood over them while they ate.

Benjie shrugged, got up and pushed his chair back.

Hal grabbed his arm. 'You'll have to take Anda!'

'No point in us both being late.'

Hal got between him and the door, made a long arm for the sliced bread on the dresser, buttered a slice and poured out a lukewarm cup of tea.

'You could've filled the pot up,' she complained.

'Let me get to the toilet,' he ducked under her arm. 'Honest – I'll wait.'

Raincoats, plastic hoods for the girls, her own school bag – Hal whirled round the flat collecting them while Benjie, as good as, but no better than his word, leaned stolidly against the door-jamb.

'The lift!' She urged him ahead, along the wide concrete balcony, exposed to lowering sky and driving rain.

In the lift, lined with corrugated metal and smelling of urine, Hal finished dressing Anda and Bell. At ground level they parted, Benjie to drop Anda at the Infants', Hal in the opposite direction making for the Catto Street Community Centre where Bell would stay till her mother picked her up at dinner-time. Savagely Hal dragged the child by the arm, jerking her like a dog on a too-short lead. Then, when Bell cried, she picked her up.

'That's enough!' Hal spoke sharply. Enough of crying, she meant. But also enough of busting herself to beat a clock that was never on her side. She was late – so what? Hal was late most days but her teacher, knowing the reason, bent the rules or not, according to her own humour. With Bell clinging to her left hip like a monkey and a heavy bag of books dragging at her right shoulder, Hal picked her way over stained, uneven pavements and puddles at an easier pace till the Centre was reached.

Retracing her steps over the canal bridge, Hal paused, leaning over the parapet, reminded of the face she had seen high up at a window in one of the houses that overlooked the site. A real face, not the face in her dream. Yet the two, in her mind, had become one and the same. Once or twice, lately, she had caught a glimpse of a curtain moving, a white blur that might have been a face. Now she knew for certain someone was there – someone who had thrown the flower-pot. She had looked up several times, after the game was over, wanting to signal her thanks for the warning. But no one had reappeared at the window. She had even, out of curiosity, counted the houses, starting at the canal end, to mark which was the right one.

The more Hal thought about the incident, the stranger it seemed. By the time she had reached the school gates she had made up her mind to go back and have another look.

The Jefferson Comprehensive was built halfway up a hill, an enormous chunky irregular building of glass and steel promontories and bays on granite slabs. 'As though to repel attack', her form mistress had once drily remarked as they walked up the slope together.

When Hal pushed through the swing doors the face at the window dropped out of her mind. Hal lived her life in separate compartments and school was one of them. The walls of the class-rooms were half-glassed, enabling any passer-by to see what was going on, and as Hal moved with animal swiftness along corridors in which the smell of polished wood-blocks competed with the smell of sweaty feet it was apparent that the morning's work was already advanced; she must be even later than usual. Some classes hummed, some droned, a few rioted. Her own class, IVb, emitted a hum which was different – the noise of people talking and arguing, animatedly but with a certain concentration.

Their room, which had been intended for use as a studio, was the height of two ordinary floors; one wall, all glass, shed a cold light on Hal's classmates, who were for the most part sitting on the floor in three groups with books, maps and drawing materials spread about them. Tables and chairs were pushed to one side. Their form-mistress, Miss Camper-down, had unconventional ideas about teaching disapproved of by the older staff who couldn't understand what she was about. But her pupils understood, and responded, on the whole, with enthusiasm.

At Hal's approach, Miss Camperdown, seated on a dais surrounded by people clamouring for guidance, looked up. She was young, of striking appearance, and casually up-to-date in her dress.

'I don't want to know,' she cut across Hal's explanation. 'So you had to take your kid sisters to school. How many others here have mothers who work? Quite frankly,' (a phrase which always preceded disapproval), 'you've done it once too often. Well haven't you?'

'Campers' didn't have a special teacher's accent, she talked like everyone else. She didn't let Hal feel she was a school kid and Campers somewhere above; you were on her level and this, combined with the sort of person she was, so far from making you free to take the mickey, made you respond in the same way. Nor, when ticked off, did you talk back for the sake of talking: it wasted time.

'I'll have to keep you in this time,' Miss Camperdown continued, 'I think the rules as silly as you do, but that's it. As much of a bind for me as you. And it only takes ten minutes extra – fifteen, perhaps.'

Hal swore she'd get up fifteen minutes earlier every day and was dismissed with a nod to the corner where her mates, preparing for a history competition, were pooling information about the slave traffic between Africa and America in the eighteenth century. IVb were divided into three groups, named by Campers, for reasons of her own which no one ever questioned, 'Levellers', 'Luddites' and 'Lollards'. They competed as hotly against each other as though they were football teams, and tended to go around together. Hal's team was the Lollards. They had to dig out their own facts, using such books as they had been able to borrow from the school or Public Library, augmented with pictures, maps and texts run off by Campers on an old duplicator in her spare time. They traced and drew and painted, and pinned the results up on screens and wall boards.

At the end of afternoon school Hal stayed behind.

'Well,' Miss Camperdown considered her with distaste, 'you've made me late for my boy-friend. I can't let him know so he'll think that I've stood him up.'

Silence followed during which Hal looked down at her toes and Miss Camperdown returned to the work she was doing. After a minute or so she resumed briskly. 'Since we've both got to stay in you may as well be useful.' For the next half-hour Hal was set to tracing maps and pictures of merchant ships in preparation for tomorrow's lesson.

'Do you have to do this every day?' Hal asked.

'You don't think my working day stops at four-fifteen?'

'I didn't know ...'

'Perhaps by the time you start to teach society will've got some of its priorities right. Till then we have to make do with too few books, not enough – too little of everything. That means extra work to help make do with what we get.'

'Teaching!' Hal was surprised. 'I never thought of being a teacher.'

'You never know.' Miss Camperdown blew away india-rubber fragments. 'Go down to the staff-room will you? Ask for two cups of tea and two buns.'

When Hal came back with the tea Miss Camperdown had her feet up on a chair and was smoking. The two drank in relaxed silence. The rain, which had beat all day against the great panes of the classroom window, had stopped. From a point midway between the expanse of water-logged sky and the grey spread of buildings, lights flashed and winked, windows caught by the westering sun, in a building like a castle.

'That's the Bute Institute!' Hal exclaimed.

'Yes,' answered Miss Camperdown, surprised by the urgency in Hal's voice, 'my boy-friend works there.'

Later, this coincidence would seem remarkable to Hal. But just now her mind was on the face at the window overlooking the Bute Street Site.

'Slaves,' Hal mused, 'there aren't any slaves now.'

'Not in this country. Not in theory anyhow.'

'In theory?'

But this was no time, Miss Camperdown realized, for a political lecture. Clearly the girl had something on her mind.

After a pause Hal continued. 'Keeping someone at the top of a house, or in a basement, say, to work for you.'

'It's been known.' Then, when Hal said nothing, staring out through the great glass panes, Miss Camperdown prompted, 'But what at – what sort of work?'

'I dunno,' Hal shrugged her shoulders. Most likely kidnappers, she thought. But the idea seemed too unrealistic – ransom, she thought, and that kid's stuff!

'What's the Bute Institute got to do with it?'

Hal looked at her. 'There's this super place,' she began, then crammed the rest of her bun into her mouth and washed it down with tea.

'Thanks for the tea,' she said when she could decently speak. 'May I go now?'

Closing the classroom door behind her Hal swallowed a final lump of bun. Cripes! In another moment she'd have come out with the lot – the site, the Game ... the site above all, the secret place. Campers was as O.K. as a teacher could be, but a teacher she was and bound, Hal reckoned, to stop kids breaking the law, even if she didn't report them to the police. And trespassing was breaking the law. Suddenly Hal cared about the site as much as she had done the first day. The threat of losing it was enough.

Hal ran down the school steps and downhill to the main crossing, where loaded buses waited for traffic lights and people hurried out of the underground, putting up umbrellas and turning up coat collars, for the rain was beginning again. Outside the butcher's men were collecting cuts of meat from shelves that jutted out among prams and dogs and shoppers. It must be near closing time, she thought – too late to get to the site. She would go tomorrow.

In the flat tea was nearly over. The whole family sat crammed into the small kitchen. The window was steamed up, the air thick with cigarette smoke and a haze of frying oil that made Hal's mouth water.

Her mother looked round as Hal came in, tired lines round her nose and down-dragged mouth, eyes half-shut against smoke from her cigarette. Before she could get the oven door open she had to shift Anda, then clear a space on the table for a plateful of sodden fish, chips and peas. There was no room to sit, so Hal ate standing up till Benjie and the little girls went into the lounge to watch telly.

Now there was more room, her father pushed his chair back. His skin shone black as coal, his eyeballs reddened with smoke and heat and because he had been up since five that morning. He was a carpenter, his work an hour's journey away.

He stirred his tea, alive to his daughter's suppressed excitement, an air of preoccupation which was strange to her.

'Where you bin?' he asked in a quiet, deep, gravelly voice.

'Kept in.' Hal washed down a lump of chips with sweet tea. Her mind was still full of the site, the mysterious face at the window, and of how she had nearly given away the whole thing to Campers.

'What for? What you done?'

'The usual – late for school.' If he says another thing, thought Hal, I'll start on about him working so far away, and Mum doing office cleaning, Anda to get to school one way, Bell another. I'll let them know. So far she never had, accepting the necessity. But if her dad sounded off about her coming home late...

Mrs Piercy turned from the sink, 'But it's after six!'

Hal replied quickly, 'She sent me for tea and buns. She's all right, Miss Camperdown. We talked...'

'What about?' Her father's suspicions were not satisfied.

'The Bute Institute.' Hal said the first thing she thought of.

'Why ever?' her mum put in.

'Her boy-friend works there. And about teaching,' she hurried on, guessing this would head them off, give them plenty to think about. 'About how I might be a teacher.' Not that she cared – teaching was the last thing Hal intended to try.

Her parents took the bait. Hal sat back while they canvassed this new idea.

'It's no surprise to me,' her father concluded, 'my uncle taught in school. Only she must work. She's always out playing.'

'No more than the others,' her mum objected.

'Clear the table,' was all her dad replied, taking out a pair of gold-rimmed spectacles.

It was the same most nights. Hal did her homework in the

kitchen, watched by her father. Benjie, when he had any to do, managed it sitting on the bed in his tiny room – enviably, being a boy, he had one to himself. But for Hal it was serious: no telly till she'd finished was the rule her dad kept her to. She got out her maths prep as being the subject he was the least likely to ask questions about. But a map of the West Indies fell out of her workbook. He leant across the table.

'Where we come from,' he said.

'I know,' she answered, though the idea was always strange to her for her mother had been born in Cardiff and the family had lived in London all her life, the first ten years of it in a basement with damp-streaked crumbling walls, and now this high flat with half London spread out beyond the windows.

'My home,' he put his thumb on the island of Barbados, and Hal gave up trying to look at figures and waited for her dad to start remembering. There wasn't much, for his own father had brought him over just before the war and then got killed, leaving six-year-old Clem Piercy to be brought up in a Home. But her dad liked remembering, specially when he was tired. The colours, the smells, the food, the sea, the people.

But tonight he only asked, 'You studying Barbados? Geography, is it?'

'Yes – well, not just that. History, too, and Science and English. All connected up, not just separate subjects. It's a new idea Miss Camperdown and some of the others have.' She looked down at her maths. 'It's too difficult to explain. You can come to the next parents' meeting.'

He continued to stare at the map. 'These marks,' he said, 'these lines and circles you've drawn.'

'It's about slavery.' She tried to keep her mind on her

maths problem. 'That's what we're learning about, got to find out about it for our next comp.'

'Slaves!' he spoke softly, 'that was us.'

Hal looked up. The idea had never struck her at school. 'It was so long ago,' she said. 'The eighteenth century, we're doing.'

'It didn't stop there,' he said. He looked down at her maths book. 'But you go on with your figures.'

He stayed quiet. Presently his head fell forward, his gold-rimmed glasses slipped. Hal finished her work, filled her school bag for next day, gently removed the glasses to safety and crept out to find her mother, half-asleep in front of the telly.

'Dad's dropped off,' she said. Soon her mother roused herself, carried first Anda, then Bell to bed, woke her husband in the kitchen and left Benjie and Hal in front of the screen till they, too, began to nod sleepily.

The last thing Hal remembered, curled up in bed, was her resolve to find Barry's house tomorrow after school.

Which means being in time, she thought, caring enough to go next door to Benjie who always woke early.

'Wake me,' she made him promise, 'just for tomorrow. I'll give you 5p.'

'You'll give me murder,' he complained sleepily, 'you know you will if I wake you.'

'Not tomorrow, honest I won't. 5p on Saturday.'

He promised.

Three

NEXT day Hal came out of school at four. She would like to have gone home to change her clothes, to make herself look more grown-up, but she couldn't risk the questions that might be asked. As she hurried to Bute Street, it rained on and off, washing the stained pavements that had suffered during the heatwave. But as she turned into the cul-de-sac sunlight broke through, intensifying the muggy heat, bringing out more children to join those already sitting on damp steps, or bicycling round and round.

Hal, swiftly counting the house-fronts from the canal-end, fixed on Number Nine as the most likely house. As she reached for the knocker, one of the cyclists whistled appreciatively and soon there was a shrill chorus. Waiting, pretending nonchalance, Hal pressed a finger into a paint blister on the brown door. She noticed an old woman lifting and dropping her yellowed lace curtain; and after she had knocked again, following the instructions on the card, she heard shuffling footsteps in the passage. With some difficulty the door was wrenched open.

It was the old woman. Peering at Hal with eyes that hardly saw, she croaked, 'You from the Welfare? You better go up. *He'll* never come down.'

From the Welfare! Hal supposed her school raincoat and the bag of books she was carrying gave her an official look. Lucky she was so tall!

'Top floor,' the old woman called after her as she mounted the stairs, '*he'll* never come down!'

But at the foot of the last flight Hal stopped, looking up. A boy, who had hastily hidden a pail behind a curtain on the landing, stood at the head of the stairs. He took a step forward and slowly came to meet her. Hal pushed back her raincoat hood and ran her hands through her hair.

Halfway down he said, 'Come up.' As he preceded her Hal saw that he held on with both hands to the shaky banister and that one foot dragged behind the other.

Once in his room she went straight to the open window. All the way up the place had smelled bad as though the yellow-brown walls, polished by countless greasy shoulders, were stewing in heat, cooking up all the odours they had absorbed in years. Bugs too – they'd come out in the heat. Hal had lived most of her life in such a place.

The room smelt better; and through the open window lay the Bute Street Site fresh from the rain.

Barry was breathing fast, painfully, partly because he had had to move around quick (for he had leant over the banister to listen when the bell had been rung and the door opened) but more from the shock of having her there, in his room. Hal moved aside as he reached the window and sat on the padded box.

'You bin ill?' she asked, seeing that he sat down because he had to, supporting himself on bone-thin arms. During his recent illness his hair had gone dull, like old straw.

He nodded, taking her in. She was more beautiful than he could have imagined, seeing her from a distance. Her skin was the colour of milky coffee, her full lips deep red, her large brown eyes as she looked at him thoughtful, considering, curious.

In fact Hal was wondering what to say next, whether to explain her visit – or indeed how to explain it at all. She felt embarrassed. Why had she come?

Barry watched the blood deepen the clear colour of her throat, her chin, her cheeks. He could not take his eyes off her. Nor could he speak.

Hal looked away; she moved round the room, noticing the pile of comics on a table that also held a washing-up bowl and cloth, turning to the padded box under the window, the gas stove in a corner. The mixture of old things and new things – the contrast between his bed with sagging springs and the record-player, between the tape-recorder on the mantelshelf and the row of grimy paperbacks leaning against it – intrigued her. All this time she was thinking what to say since he wouldn't or perhaps couldn't speak.

At last she began, 'I thought – I came to see – there seemed to be – isn't there anyone with you?' She glanced at the door in the back wall opposite the window.

Barry shook his head. He was beginning to breathe easier now and the fear that he might be sick had worn off. 'Mum works. She comes back to give me my dinner.'

'When does she get back in the evenings?' Hal asked nervously, not ready to explain herself to any grown-up, least of all the boy's mum.

'Not for an hour or so, yet. She does a bit of overtime. If she hasn't got a customer coming here, that is. She does dress-making at home as well.'

'What's your name?' she asked, sitting on the edge of the box. 'Mine's Hal Piercy.'

'Barry Padgitt. That's a boy's name – Hal?'

Hal laughed it off: 'Short for Hallelujah!'

'You kidding?'

'My real name is Gloria. It's Dad. He's got funny ideas about names – romantic, sort of. At least, for girls. Fancy names like Amanda and Bella – my kid sisters, we call them Anda and Bell. And me – being called Gloria, at school they called me Glory, and one day our teacher said "Hallelujah!" She thought it was funny. I minded at the time, I was just a kid, and of course all the other kids yelled out "Hallelujah!" not knowing what it meant.'

'What *does* it mean?'

Hal thought. 'I dunno. Anyhow they all went round shouting it.'

'And it got shortened to Hal. Hal,' he tried it out, looking at her. 'I like it. It's all right. Suits you.'

'What school d'you go to?' Hal asked.

'I don't,' Barry said, his pallor noticeably flushing, and hurried on. 'They said I wasn't to – at the hospital.' This wasn't true.

'What did you have wrong?'

'They never said. Real bad, I was. They took pints and pints of blood. The students come every day and took the blood.' Barry liked talking about his illness. 'I nearly died,' he lied again. He looked sidelong at Hal to see if she believed him. From her thoughtful expression he could not tell.

'How long ago?' she asked. 'How long, I mean, since you come out?'

'I forget,' Barry said, and this was true, more or less, for all days seemed the same. 'Just before we come here.'

Not wanting her to ask any more questions, he got up and opened the door into his mother's room. 'I'll have a look to see if Mum's on her way,' he said, to change the subject.

'I better go,' Hal said quickly.

'No – please!' Barry's voice was urgent. 'She won't be here yet.'

Because he still held the door open Hal walked through, fascinated by what she could see beyond – the bright materials draped on a dressmaker's dummy, flung over chairs, spilling from drawers, the dresses hanging from the picture rail, the vases of plastic and paper flowers. And the photographs, dozens of them, plain and coloured, stuck round the mirror and about the room, all of a little boy wearing different clothes, suits, coats or blouses and short pants, taken at different ages.

The boy looked so unnaturally clean, his fair hair brushed, his clothes new, not a button, a velvet cuff or a bow tie out of place. Very out-of-date they all were, photos of a child model advertising clothes, or sometimes things like groceries and soap. Looking closer she saw most of the pictures were cut from magazines. She wondered at Barry's mum wanting all those pictures around of the same, doll-like boy. Perhaps a kid that had died? It gave her the creeps.

'That was years ago,' he said, embarrassed. And added more hopefully, 'I bin on telly – twice.'

Hal looked at him. 'That you?' she asked incredulously.

He nodded; and Hal, now, could just see in the dun straw hair, the whey-white cheeks and narrow shoulders, the ghost of the child in the photographs.

She took a deep breath. 'I like you better the way you are now.'

'They make me sick!' Barry said violently, turning his back on the pictures and going over to the window. 'I stopped doing it – modelling – when I was about eight.'

He sat slumped on the edge of his mother's machine table,

one leg out like a prop. When he spoke again it was flatly, defensively, 'I don't see how anyone could.'

'I suppose you had to, if you were just a kid. You must've made a packet – your mum must've.'

'I don't mean being a model – I mean what you said.'

'What I said?'

'I don't see how anyone could like me.'

Hal, who had been turning a plastic ornament over and over, put it back on the crowded shelf.

'Come on out,' she said abruptly, staring at the ornament, a mermaid with seaweed across her breasts sitting on a rock. 'We could go out the back way on to the site.'

She couldn't see Barry's face, backed by the light, but when he spoke the fear in his voice as he croaked, 'No!' brought back her earlier ideas about his being kept here by force.

'Why not?'

'I can't.'

'You mean you never ...?'

'With Mum, sometimes.'

'Then you can come with me. You won't have to walk far. I'll get you over the wall somehow. There'd be a box or something.'

Hal had walked through into the back room and was looking out over the site. He'd never get well in this stuffy old room smelling of women's sweat and stale cigarette ends. His mum must be ... Her imagination failed. Mad? She couldn't think of any reason for keeping a sick boy up here.

'C'm on!' she urged him, holding out her hand. 'Got a raincoat? The ground'll be wet.'

Barry sat astride a chair. 'You don't understand ...'

She had begun to frighten him, standing over him, ready to spring. He put his head on his arms.

'Go on,' she said gently, 'tell me. Why won't your mum – '

'It's got nothing to do with her,' he said wearily. 'I just can't – '

'Then what's stopping you?'

Desperately he tried: 'The doctor.'

'Doctor?' she cried suspiciously, 'I don't believe you've seen a doctor!'

Furious, now, she swept up her raincoat and made for the door.

'Do me a favour!' she cried. 'You don't fancy coming out. O.K. Sorry I asked. But doctors – you don't have to bring them in! As though any doctor...'

He raised his head with an effort. 'Come back,' he managed to say. 'Please – tomorrow.'

He spoke so low she had to come close and listen.

'I wanted to ask you – there's so much – you'll never start it again, will you?'

He looked a sort of blue colour round the mouth; Hal was afraid to leave him.

'What d'you mean?' she said. Barry went over to his bed and lay down with his hands behind his head.

'The Game. You won, didn't you? And that finished it.'

Hal came and sat down on the bed. For the first time she felt more certain they were talking about the same thing.

'Hadn't thought about it,' she said. 'Well, hardly at all. The rain came... I dunno. Shouldn't think we ever will play any more. It was a kid's game, anyhow. But what makes you so sure?' She hurriedly repeated, 'It was a kid's game. Y'know? There was a teacher, at my last school, used to take us out on the heath. That was before we moved into the flat. And she played this kid's game with us – "Flags", she called it. There's nowhere to play now, near the flats. Then one day Benjie and I – he's my brother – came down the canal with Anda and Bell and another girl with *her* kid sister and brother, and we saw this hole in the wall – see? Well, not a hole –'

'A gap between the wall and the end garden.' Barry cut in animatedly, 'and you squeezed through and found – all that,' he gestured towards the window and the site.

'You *saw* us?'

'Not the first day – not the day you found the site. But I can just – the place is real good, isn't it? When I first saw you – the day after we moved in here – you were playing this game – Flags, is it?'

'That's what our teacher in the Juniors called it. But I'm telling you – it's a kid's game. I started it for something to do – for Anda, my brother Benjie and other kids. There's quite a few of us from the flats has kid sisters and brothers, and the park's miles, and the ground round the flats is real grotty, so when we found the Bute Street place ...'

Barry nodded. His blue colour had changed. Hal, bent on making sure Barry didn't think she played games like Flags for her own fun, insisted, 'It was a swell place. After a bit I remembered this kid's game –'

'And after a bit the game changed,' Barry nodded again. 'But how did the Span – guys that got in from the other end – were they the same lot as yours?'

Hal shook her head. 'Crimp Watson, he found the site, too. Not so soon as us, but pretty soon. He and his gang, some of them, had kids they had to bring along with them, like we did. They watched us playing and began to join in.'

'It didn't happen at once, the change. But you kept on making new rules –'

'I don't know that we actually *said* –'

'But things happened.' Barry remembered Anda and Bell.

'It stopped being just a kid's game. You'd take the really young ones into the jun – well, it *was* like a jungle – to safety before it started.'

'Hey!' Hal cried, 'not so much about safety. No one got hurt.'

'But it wasn't exactly a kid's game any more. Those fights in No-man's-land ...'

'It wasn't bad fun,' Hal got up. 'But it wasn't like you think. I mean we didn't *plan* anything.' She was amazed at Barry's knowing so much, even though he'd got it mostly wrong; she was astonished at his caring the way he did. 'To think of you up here all the time. You could've come down,' she had forgotten their earlier quarrel. 'All those fine days,' she said, feeling pity for him.

'It was the fine weather that did it,' he said. 'D'you know, it never rained for three weeks? So you came out every day, more and more of you ...'

'We wanted more people. But we didn't want to tell everyone, 'cause of keeping the site a secret.'

'Hundreds of people must know about it.'

'Not so many. There are houses all round, and the Institute one end and the canal wall the other. We'll be stopped in the end though. The cops'll get us.'

'You'll come back, then?'

'Sure. But you're right about the Game. That's finished, though how you knew ...'

'The Sp – Crimp Watson. You'll never get *him* out again. He was mad at being beaten. And by a girl, too.'

Hal grinned happily at the memory of that last fight.

'What happened afterwards? I didn't see that. After you'd got him down and over the boundary.'

Boundary – Hal wondered at all the terms he used, he'd got the whole thing taped, whereas down there ... 'In a war,' she said, 'you don't have names for everything. Things just happen. No plans. Before, perhaps, and afterwards. But at the time ... Anyhow,' she heaved herself off the wall where she'd been leaning, 'the Game's over. Not because of Crimp. It's just – well – over.'

'If you started again it would be just a kid's game?'

'Yeah – I dunno,' she said impatiently, 'it's over, that's all.' She picked up her bag and raincoat for the second time.

'One thing's for sure,' Barry said, getting up and going over to the window. 'Crimp Watson'll never come back to Bute Street!' He meant to compliment Hal; but she opened the door as if to end their talk.

'You'll come back?' he begged.

'I'll be bringing the kids to the site.'

'No – up here. Please?'

She considered him. 'Not if you won't come down.' Now that the door was open the full stench from the stairway nauseated her. 'Come out the back,' she finally offered, 'next time you see us out there. I'll get you over the wall somehow.'

She waited. But her pity, her curiosity, and something more, the sense of a deeper understanding between them – all were overborne by his miserable silence.

She flung out and ran downstairs, not touching the walls, holding her breath.

After she had gone, Barry stared out over the Bute Street Site. It hadn't been much use, talking to Hal about the Game. For him she was still two people: the Indian Queen who had inhabited the secret ways of the jungle; and the girl who had just left him. Both were gone. Of the two he minded the loss of the real girl less.

He looked at his watch. It was about time for his mother to come home. From her window at the front of the house he could lean out and watch Hal turn the street corner. He quickly drew back, seeing the boys still cycling aimlessly round the street below. They seemed to him like vultures circling in the sky, waiting for him. For, most of all, Barry was afraid of other boys.

He went and lay face downward on his bed. Soon the street door slammed. He could hear his mother complaining as she climbed four steep flights of stairs.

She was still complaining as she flung open the door. 'Caught me ankle on that useless bike in the passage – there it stands, in the way, never used, still paying for it, them special gears and that horn and all.'

'I never asked you to buy it.' Barry turned over on his back, arms behind his head, watching her move about the room, clearing a space for the food she'd brought in, kicking off her shoes, dropping cigarette ash everywhere.

He sat up, and she, throwing a cigarette-end into a bucket where it sizzled, came down and sat beside him, her weight bouncing him up on the noisy springs. He saw her face close to, large, anxious, her eye-brows plucked to nothingness making way for pencilled orange ones to match her frizzed-up hair, as he was taken into her soft embrace.

Mrs Padgitt didn't ask Barry what he had done since dinner-time, when she had come back from her work-place with fish and chips for them both. She would have been afraid to ask, knowing his answer would be, 'nothing', with a hollow look in his drawn face which would be more than she could bear. Barry had never told her about the children, still less would he have told her about the Indian Queen.

Mrs Padgitt rarely looked out at the site, and if, this evening, she had, she would have seen it empty: the children had all gone home.

She got up, lit another cigarette, and resumed her quiet nagging as she moved about preparing supper. He could at least have done the potatoes, she complained, taking the bowl to fill at the landing tap. She complained about the bucket, too. Barry used this rather than go down the steep stairs to the toilet outside more often than he had to. This habit had begun when he was too ill to go; now – well, he was lazy, every movement was still an effort, and then there were all the others who lived in the house. Barry hated meeting them, putting up with their remarks, either of pity or curiosity or hostility. His mother grumbled, but she took the bucket with a cloth over it down all those stairs and out into the yard. She came back breathless, to find that Barry had let the potatoes boil over.

'You lie there,' she cried, 'you never lift a finger!' She made a little rush at him, like a hen going for another hen, and Barry automatically put his arm across his face. But she wouldn't hit him, he knew that. He only had to put on a wan expression and suck in his cheeks to make himself seem worse, to have her worried face close to and another hot hug.

They ate their supper, mostly out of tins, on a table that was almost too small to hold it. They quarrelled because he didn't finish his plate of stew, but almost in the same breath she was chattering on about what had happened at work, what Mr So-and-so had said and what *she'd* said, while she opened a tin of pineapples, lit another cig, poured water from the kettle into the bowl, pulled her tight dress over her head and washed under her arms while her cig burnt in a saucer.

'I'm in a hurry tonight,' she said, going to her room. 'Mrs Roebuck's coming.'

Barry finished the pineapple and two cup cakes. His mother was always in a rush. She was a good dressmaker, and though only two months had passed since their move here, smart cars were already to be seen parked outside their house two or three evenings a week. Because she kept her charges low.

'I'm "the little woman round the corner",' she cried contemptuously, but with a touch of pride. 'That's what they call me. "My dear, I've found the most *mahvellous* little woman!".'

She came back as she spoke. Barry had to laugh, her voice was so like Mrs Roebuck's. Not that he ever saw these ladies; his mother hid him when they came, ashamed or guilty, above all afraid of the fuss there would be if it was discovered that he existed, and wouldn't leave the house or start going to a new school.

'That's her!' she exclaimed, hearing the two double knocks that meant Top Floor. She hurried out, pulling the curtain that hid the landing tap, clip-clopping down the lino stairs in her sling-back heels, and after a while Barry heard them both return and enter his mother's room by the other door. With the high sound of their chatter Barry's sense of isolation returned; he hated these women who took up his mother's time.

He went back to his window, pulled himself up on the box and leant out. It was still light, but a thick, shadowy light, full of the smells of blistered paint, trodden grass, canal water, and fried food drifting through open windows.

As Barry sniffed, hoping for a fresh breeze, he saw a movement at the Institute end of the site.

What he saw there made him sit up. A man was leaning over the wall, talking to a group of boys. One of them turned, waving an arm towards the 'jungle'. It was the Spaniard – unmistakable in his bush hat, in spite of the shadows. The man put a leg over the wall and jumped down to join them.

A cop – fuzz in plain clothes! Barry remembered Hal's words. 'We'll be stopped in the end.' So this was Crimp's revenge – making sure Hal never got back to the site, or if she did that she'd be copped.

And Barry didn't know where she lived. If he had, he'd have got to her somehow. For the first time since they'd come here, Barry's room, which had been his safety, felt like a prison, himself a prisoner, and his own jailer.

Four

On Saturday Mrs Piercy cleaned the flat. Hal, sooner than help, took Anda and Bell down to the concrete playground attached to the flats. There were concrete drainpipes, odd-shaped concrete blocks to climb on, a big concrete railway engine you could sit in, and space to whizz around these obstacles on small bikes, trikes, etc. But Anda and Bell had nothing on wheels and got bored clambering about the Mappin Terrace of the play-space. It was sunk a little below ground-level and consequently airless. Hal sat on a concrete bench reading a comic.

'Why don't you take us to the Secret Place?' Anda kept on at her.

'Secret Place!' Bell echoed. She didn't talk much.

Hal had been trying not to think of the site, because it reminded her of Barry. Somehow, the place had been spoiled for her. She turned on Anda, 'If you say that again I'll smack your bottom!'

'Lollies!' yelled the girls when the ice-cream van came round. But Hal had no money for lollies.

Then Bell was knocked down by a boy on a trike. As Hal rocked and comforted her baby sister, absently, like a bored but affectionate mother, Anda came to be comforted too. She put her head down on Hal's knee.

'Why can't we go back?' she wailed.

Hal, who had occasionally asked herself this question without getting much of an answer, looked thoughtfully at Anda. She was not used to questioning her motives. You either did a thing or you didn't. All she knew was that this boy Barry – the way he looked, the way he lived – sickened her. And when she thought about the Bute Street Site this sick feeling seemed to have spread all over that too. But, looking at Anda, Hal's sensible mind rebelled: how could a boy, how could anyone spoil a *place?*

'We'll go – some time soon.'

But all Sunday passed by without Hal making up her mind.

Monday – after school – she'd go for certain.

But on Monday something unusual happened: Hal's school was given a whole holiday because someone had won a scholarship.

It felt strange, running down the school steps into the June sunshine, with that early-morning-after-breakfast feeling still in her tummy. Hal came down in a rush, along with a crowd of her classmates.

'Hey' – shouted a boy, 'You – Hal! Why don't we go back to the Bute Street Site?' Hal didn't like him much, but she liked his sister, Betty Pratt, who had been one of the chosen band Hal had told about her discovery of the site. Then, when they wanted more people for the game that had become a battle, her brother Kevin, young but strong, had been roped in.

A group of boys and girls collected round her.

'Not me,' she said. If she went back at all, she wanted to go alone. 'Haven't any of you been back?'

Somehow, no one had.

'It was you who fixed it,' a girl said, shrugging her shoulders, 'the Game.'

'Didn't you say we wouldn't be playing the Game any more?' asked another.

'It was a kid's game anyway,' said a dark, rather plump boy, Dimitri Georgiou. He and his brother Andreas were almost like twins, though Dimitri was nearly a year older. Hal liked them better than any of the other boys in IVb.

It seemed clear that no one else was interested in the Bute Street Site as a place on its own – a place to go with trees and grass and wildness. This thought was a relief to Hal as she walked to the school gates with a couple of girl friends, Betty Pratt and Mary Malone. At the gate three older boys waited uncertainly.

'Coming out tonight?' asked one. 'There's a Western on at the Odeon.'

'Not a hope,' Betty Pratt said.

'We could meet at my place,' Mary suggested. 'You coming, Hal?'

'I might.' But she knew she wouldn't. It would mean asking her mother for money. *And* get by her dad and his passion for her homework. For such reasons Hal went out less often than her friends. But this didn't stop people – fellows and girls – wanting her to come out with them. Her aloofness, had she known it, was part of her attraction. As Betty said, 'It's just *because* – because you play it so cool.'

The three girls, Hal in the middle, were on their way down the hill towards the traffic lights. Betty, round-shouldered, her yellow hair cut short so that her head looked like a small round flower on a nodding stalk, was the tallest; but Hal, straight-backed, with a spine that flexed like an animal's as she walked, dominated the group. Mary, small and compact, her coppery hair in a snakey tangle of curls, bobbed along, taking two steps to their one. The three had been friends since their first term, though they saw little of one another out of school. And lately there'd been the Bute Street Site.

'T'is the way she looks.' Mary enviously scrutinized her freckles and grey-green eyes in a pocket mirror.

'She makes things happen, like the Game.'

'D'you mind,' Hal interjected, 'it's me you're talking about!'

'It was fab while it lasted,' Mary sighed, 'the Game!'

'Yes,' Betty agreed, 'but it couldn't've gone on. Some of Crimp Watson's lot were really rough.'

'Funny,' said Mary regretfully, 'we don't know where any of them live. They can't come from round here. We never see any of them, y'know, in the caffs and that. There was one feller ...'

'C'mon!' Betty put her arm round Hal's waist. 'We ought to do something new – something really good, Hal – what shall we do? Right *now?*'

'I'm going home,' Hal detached herself as they reached the traffic lights. She'd been on the point of suggesting that the three of them should go along to the Bute Street Site. But she knew, if she went at all, she must first go back alone. It was that creep Barry who'd spoiled everything. Always there, looking down. Now that she'd seen the place from his window the very memory was spoiled.

Back in the empty flat Hal changed her school clothes for her jeans and a bright pink shiny shirt patterned with scarlet and orange whorls. Through her bedroom window a grey haze muffled streets and skyscrapers, softened the far pinnacles of the rail terminus. Rails, acres and acres of them, gleamed dully; a diesel hooted, gathered speed, disappeared in a tunnel followed by interminable trucks. All around the quietness of the flat radios in other flats sang out the same song. It was the quietness, the emptiness that got Hal, alone so strangely in the middle of the morning. The flat, as she passed open doors in the hallway, looked different, waiting for people to come back, for her mum, in particular, to tidy up, get the tea, polish the reddened doorstep, water the flower-box outside.

She shut the door behind her and the noise reverberated along the wide concrete gallery. Mrs Lattice, two doors down, came out to shake a mat over the balcony. 'You sick or somthin'? Your mum – she sick?'

Hal shook her head. 'Got a school holiday.'

Mrs Lattice gave her a sharp look; clearly she didn't believe Hal.

As Hal neared Bute Street, past the butcher's shop with meat on trestles jutting out among the children and prams and dogs, past the greengrocer's sparse, shrivelled cabbages and whitening pea-pods, she experienced a moment of near-panic; she was uncertain what she meant to do, and this, for Hal, was a most unusual situation. She didn't want to turn up into Bute Street itself, that's for sure! She made her way to the canal towpath, past the canal basin choked with a variety of craft floating or half-sinking in stages of disrepair. The canal ran between a high, blank warehouse wall and the wall of the Bute Street Site.

Hal squeezed through the gap and stood without moving, breathing more and more easily as she took in the familiar contours, bushes, grass, tree-crowned heights, and gulleys deep in yellow, white and purple flowers.

Hal thought of Anda's name for it: 'The Secret Place'.

She, Hal, must've been crazy to think that anything could spoil it!

She walked on, coming to the big open space where fights had taken place, careful not to look towards Barry's window, willing herself not to think about him or his miserable room. Instead she remembered Crimp Watson in their last fight, and how she had tricked him by going limp then suddenly, with all her strength, heaving him off and rolling him over. But this reminded her of the flowerpot – if Barry hadn't warned her she'd have been Crimp's prisoner.

And so, at last, Hal turned about and looked up at the window.

It was blank; no face looked out.

Hal felt relieved and disappointed and alarmed all at once, the boy must be really ill – too ill to sit at the window!

It was now that she heard a noise; something was being pulled, dragged, scraped over concrete. The noise was slow and somehow painful; it went on for a long time, and Hal thought, it's coming from Barry's garden!

Two hands gripped the top of the garden wall; and Barry's head appeared.

'Hullo!' said Hal, her voice bright with surprise and relief.

'You shouldn't be here!'

'D'you mind!' Hal was outraged by his cheek. 'We're having a school holiday, not that it's anything to do with you!'

'I came down here to warn you, you can't come here any more – the cops know. That feller you licked – Crimp. Crimp told them everything –' he finished dramatically. 'Bet it was revenge. Because of your beating him!'

'Crimp?' Hal said incredulously, 'Crimp Watson?' She

came and stood close to the wall. 'He can't have,' she concluded. 'How would you know, anyway?'

'I saw him.'

Hal hesitated, divided between feelings of repulsion and curiosity – curiosity, not about Crimp, for she was convinced Barry was making the whole unlikely story up, but about Barry himself.

'Come on down,' she said. The wall on her side was shoulder-high. Barry shook his head, sick with fear and shame.

'Yes!' she fiercely insisted, and gripped his wrists.

For a long minute they stared at one another. Her chin was up, her jaw-line hard, her dark red lips close and firm, her brown eyes – the look in her eyes terrified, compelled and drew him.

Her grip tightened on his wrists. With infinite effort Barry got one leg up along the wall, then the other leg.

'You don't have to jump,' she said, 'just let yourself down.' Barry scraped, scrambled and fell, taking her with him, into the shallow ditch below the wall.

Hal extricated herself, sat up and watched him. Exasperated yet anxious, she burst out, 'You can *move*, can't you?'

Barry got to his feet and walked a few steps over the grass. He knelt down and touched it, still cool from last night's dew. He ran his palm over it; his fair hair fell over his cheek.

Hal wished he would look up; she wanted him to see the leaves, the flowers, the little hills, the saplings on those hills, motionless under the sun's light, except when a breeze turned the leaves back, skimmed over the bushes, shivered the flowering grasses.

After a while he turned over and lay on his back, his arms outstretched, looking up at the sky.

'O.K.?' Hal said at last, wanting to talk, not knowing how to begin.

Barry propped himself up on his elbows, looked at her and smiled. It was the first time Hal had seen him smile. It gave her a feeling of triumph, as though she had made him do it, the way she had made him jump off the wall.

'It's funny, seeing you down here,' he said.

'Funny?'

'I mean it *feels* funny – being out here with you.'

'Anything'd feel funny after being up there for so long. I don't understand . . .'

'Well, I'm here now.' Barry got to his feet. 'Why don't we look around? Can I – could you show me – I mean, would you mind if we went into the jungle?' He nodded his head towards the bushes.

'Is that what you call it? Not much like a jungle!'

'That's how I thought of it. There must be hundreds of tunnels.'

'It's a bit scratchy. Anyhow, there's nothing to see. I might tear my shirt.'

'It's super,' he said, sitting down, hugging his knees, 'the colour of the shirt an' all.'

Hal had never had a boy pass a remark on her clothes before. She supposed it was on account of his mum making dresses.

'We'll go into the tunnels another time,' she said, 'but you ought to walk around a bit'. She glanced at his stick-like legs. 'Get used to walking.'

As she led him over the grassy space, with its dips and hillocks, that Barry had called 'No-man's-land', he forgot his wobbly knees and aching back. Looking sideways at Hal,

Barry knew that he could never tell her the name he had once given her.

'It looks much bigger from down here,' he said, 'but so does everything, the hills and trees and that.'

They walked round the undergrowth on Crimp's side, making for his hideout on its hillock. This was a ruined bay window, once part of a large house.

'It's nothing like as good as your hideout,' Barry said, 'I could see that from up there. For one thing you can see exactly where it is. For another, you'd only have to get round behind and you'd be there – it's right on the edge of the cover.'

'That's what I was trying to do, that time you threw the flowerpot.' Hal looked at Barry, 'That was real nice of you.'

'I didn't want you to be caught. But I didn't want the Game to end. I'd sort of thought it'd go on for ever.'

'Well it did end,' Hal spoke dismissively. 'And about time. It was a kid's game, like I said. Have a look at this,' she went on, climbing up to the ruin.

Inside the half-circle of brick there were rough benches, an old oil-drum, lolly-sticks and other signs of occupation. They looked through the empty window-frame at Crimp's lookout tree, one of the few fully-grown trees on the site.

'It's a sycamore, I think,' Barry said. 'There were lots of them in a field near our house.'

'Was it the country, then?'

'Not proper. But ours was the end house. There was a stream, too.'

'Why did you leave?'

Barry shrugged his shoulders. 'Something happened while I was in hospital, I suppose. The day before I come out, Mum told me we were moving. Could be Mum got bored by Mr Barnes, the manager of the Co-op. Dead keen on Mum, he was. Wanted to marry her.' He looked at Hal with a certain pride. 'It's not the first time. She's not bad-looking, even at her age. But she never does – get married, I mean. Dunno why.' He reflected and went on. 'But I shouldn't think it was that. Mr Barnes used to give us credit, more than Mum could pay back. Yeah, it was the money, more likely. It's much cheaper here, anyway.'

'It should be!' Hal looked up at the house-backs, some with cracks in the walls, all in disrepair. 'They ought to be pulled down and flats built.'

'I'd hate to live in one of them new flats, high up, and no grass or trees.'

'You should see ours!'

Hal told Barry about the flat, and about the basement where they'd all been squashed in before. 'The only decent thing about it was it was near the heath.'

She told him about Benjie, Anda and Bell, and how she had to take the kids to school and day-nursery and how that made her late. She told him about the school and Miss Camperdown.

'You'd like our school,' she said, 'it's not half bad. Shall I ask her if you can come? She'd fix it with Mr Beach – the headmaster.'

'I can't.' All Barry's fears returned, and Hal saw again the pinched, grey look on his face.

'Why?'

But Barry only shook his head and looked away.

'Go on,' she said, 'you can tell me. I won't tell anyone else, cross my heart. Why can't you come to school? Is it your mum won't let you? She'll have to, you know. They send someone round if you don't come.' Hal thought for a moment and went on, 'I don't know why they haven't already. P'raps they did, and you wouldn't open the door? You know that old girl downstairs? She thought I was from the Welfare!'

Hal laughed at the recollection. But Barry was far from laughing. And Hal's laugh didn't last long.

'If you don't tell me,' she said, 'I'll never come back. Honest, I didn't mean to after last time, kidding me about "what the doctor said". There's not much wrong with you, not now there isn't.'

She had forgotten that she had only come back to take a look at the Bute Street Site, not to see Barry. Now that she *had* seen him her curiosity was stronger than ever. And not just curiosity; some feeling, part pity, part resentment – for she could sense that the very fact that he existed, miserably, alone, would nag and spoil her own life, as it had nagged her these last few days. And there was the sensation of power too: she had got him out, she had got him over the wall. She couldn't stop at that. 'Go on!' She leant forward, fixing him with her eyes.

'You won't understand,' he said. But what did it matter? She wouldn't want to see him again anyway. 'I don't mind what you know,' he said. 'It's because I'm scared – scared to go out. I feel ill the moment I do.'

'But you didn't with me.'

'I do now.' Barry put his head in his hands. He waited for her to go.

Hal waited, not knowing what to do. Then she said: 'We better go back.'

When they got to the wall they found Barry was too weak to climb it.

'Before I was ill I could've shinned up easy,' he gasped, after Hal had pushed and he had scrambled in vain.

Hal said, 'It's no good. We'll have to go round the front.'

'I can't,' he said, 'I can't.'

'You'll have to.' She held out her hand.

When he still hung back she spoke sharply, 'You go out with your mum, you say? You can go back with me!'

She took his hand. Barry was surprised that her hand felt cool; he had imagined it would be hot.

She began to walk, drawing him after her. Every so often she would look back at him, and the look on her face, which had got him over the wall in the first place, now got him to the gap between the canal wall and the gardens.

Five

SUDDENLY the gap was filled! It was her brother Benjie, and after him Kevin, and Betty and Mary – the whole gang! For a moment no one spoke, astonishment and curiosity striking the newcomers dumb. Then Hal got out, 'This is Barry.'

'Hya, Barry,' Mary greeted him, appraising Barry with her grey-green eyes. Looking at Hal with her wide, red curly smile she began, 'And isn't she the deep one? Not a word to anyone . . .'

'Stuff it!' Hal would have hit Mary in the mouth to stop her going on. 'He got over the wall – see? He couldn't get back. He's been ill.'

In a few minutes everyone was helping Barry over his wall.

Till then Barry had been speechless. But, astride the wall, he waved dramatically towards the Institute: 'See there! What did I tell you? Crimp's split on you. The cops – you best run *now* – I'll keep 'em talking!'

One or two turned and made for the gap. But Hal and her friends stood their ground, Hal with her thumbs stuck in her belt.

'Nurts!' said Hal, narrowing her eyes to see if it really was Crimp Watson who was leading the approaching group. So far as she could see there was only one grown-up with them.

'I'd just like to hear what Crimp's bin saying – I'd just like to hear!'

Crimp came up, and Hal guessed from his red face and the way he stared fixedly at the top of her head that the circumstances of their last meeting still rankled.

But all he said, with a jerk of his thumb, was, 'He wants to talk to you.'

'Hullo!' the man greeted them. 'I've seen you here quite a bit. I work at the Institute.'

'Yeah?' Hal was non-committal.

Barry hissed from over his wall, 'He's kidding you. 'Course he doesn't work there!'

Hal looked at the man. His eyes were deep blue, his skin pale, as though he didn't get out much. His ginger beard ran from ear to ear, outlining a firm chin. Hal didn't fancy beards, but she responded to his smile, which seemed particularly directed at her.

'He wants,' Crimp said tentatively, 'to start an ad – what you call it?' He knew quite well, but he wanted the Institute bloke to put the idea across. What little he knew of Hal – in the way that an army commander gets to know his enemy – made him fairly certain she would oppose it.

'Not me,' the man said hastily, 'I'm not starting anything. It's something you'll have to do for yourselves, if you want to. Do you know anything about adventure playgrounds?'

Everyone shook their heads. Everyone, that is, except Barry, who kept pointedly out of the discussion.

'I don't either, much,' the young man went on. 'It just seems to me that this place is wasted. You could do a lot with it. From time to time a bunch of kids come along, mess around for a spell, get fed up – I don't know why. But I've been watching from up there. It's the only open space for miles around.'

'Yeah,' Crimp agreed. 'There's no parks.'

'It wouldn't be like an ordinary playground,' the man went on. 'You could make anything you wanted of it.'

'Football pitches,' Crimp said.

'Two five-a-sides,' added young Benjie.

'There'd be room for that. Though there's not much level ground. Most of it we – you'd leave wild the way it is. There'd have to be a hut, for other recreations and wet days – that could go up our end.'

The man waited, looking at Hal.

'I don't fancy it,' she said, and turned away.

'We'll do it without you!' Crimp shouted.

'Who'd ever let us?' objected Benjie, attracted nevertheless by the promise of football pitches.

'The land belongs to the railway,' the man said, 'they can't do anything with it except keep people off it –'

'Which they can't do,' Crimp put in, 'not without having a copper on duty day and night.'

'Look,' the man continued, 'I'd like to help, I really would.' He sounded disappointed, Hal thought, like a kid who's been promised a treat and let down.

'Think about it,' he said, when she turned back to look at him. 'Crimp Watson here says he will. I know his name but I don't know yours. Mine's Tim Black.'

'She's Hal,' Benjie for once took the lead. 'I'm Benjie, there's Anda and Bell and Mary and Betty and Kevin ... but they're not our family.' He looked at Barry. 'And he's ...'

They all looked at Barry, head and shoulders over the wall.

'I'm not in this,' muttered Barry, and disappeared.

'Why not?' Hal shouted, suddenly furious. 'I don't mind coming along,' she said, loud enough for him to hear.

'He's a nutcase!' Crimp had just worked out that Barry must've thrown the fatal flowerpot.

Hal took three steps towards Crimp. 'D'you mind?'

'Any friend of yours ...' Crimp sneered in mock politeness.

'O.K.,' the man hurriedly interposed, 'why don't we have a look round?' As they moved off towards the Institute he went on, 'The railway people'll let us use the site. They seemed quite keen to have it used. There's not much they can do because of the ground beneath being honeycombed with tunnels.'

'A car park?' Crimp Watson put in.

'Too much ups and downs,' said Kevin.

'Too much ups and downs for pitches?' This from Benjie.

'We'll level a part of it for that,' Tim answered.

'Need a bulldozer,' said Crimp.

'Crimp's ol' man runs a plant hire firm, mister!'

'Need a bulldozer,' said Crimp.

Tim, who had a clip-board, made a note on it, sitting on the low Institute wall. 'The Council'll provide a hut for wet weather. They'll start us with tools and a load of wood – odd stuff from demolished houses.'

'For the hut?'

'No. That'll be done by builders.'

'What for, then?'

'To build – anything you like.'

The older children were silent, incredulous, suspicious. What was the catch?

'Well – how about it?' When no one spoke, he went on, 'The Institute here are willing to let you have their garden.'

Behind him were neglected overgrown flowerbeds and bushes, an old shed, a glasshouse with broken panes. 'You could grow things, those that want to. Keep rabbits – other animals and birds. It'd be a safe place for the small kids, with a sand-pit, and maybe a helper to look after them.' He sized them up, undecided, still suspicious as they were, saying with a smile, 'That'd let some of you baby-minders off the hook.'

There were one or two answering smiles and a small, approving murmur.

He looked down at Crimp, then over to Hal who stood a little apart, with Anda and Mary, the two Greek boys and others from her school. 'It's up to you,' he said.

Just then Hal, uncertain what to say, heard a noise behind. She turned to see Barry behind her.

'He came over the wall!' cried Anda.

Barry stood looking at Hal. The two of them were taller than the others and could be seen by every eye that turned in their direction. As though there was no one else there, Barry addressed her, 'You don't have to.'

'Keep out of this!' she muttered angrily, and turned back to look across at Tim. 'I don't mind if we do,' she cried.

After that her schoolmates began to talk eagerly among themselves. Similarly, Crimp's lot gathered round him. Tim jumped off the wall and moved among the children. In his tight jeans he had a loping gait like a cowboy, and a quick jerky movement of his head as he responded to their questions.

'Hey, mister!' Mary called him over. 'We're never going to be let do this on our own?'

'No,' said Tim. 'You'll want a play-leader. I thought I'd apply for the job if the thing gets going – the adventure playground. My work at the Institute finishes soon.'

'Ah well,' Mary gave him a questing look from under her dark lashes, 'that's different, isn't it?'

Tim looked past her as though wanting to speak to Hal. But Hal, for some reason she could not have explained, felt suddenly shy, and turned away. Betty lingered at her side; and Mary, bubbling with curiosity, stood in front of her, hands thrust deep in the pocket of her plastic raincoat, her freckled nose wrinkled as though sniffing the air.

'Isn't she the deep one,' she crowed, '*two* fellers, and no one the wiser! The ginger one, now, with them deep, deep blue eyes . . . Tim, did he say?'

'*I don't know him,*' Hal muttered through her teeth.

As to Barry, who now lay propped up on one arm, listening intently, she was ready to disown him, too.

'And the fair one,' Mary pursued, 'him with eyes like cats.'

'Get this,' Hal was desperate, 'I don't know him either. He had got over the wall on to the site. He couldn't get back.' It was more or less true.

'He knows *you* all right.'

'What was that he said?' Betty asked jealously. 'What did he mean : "You needn't if you don't want to"?'

'He's a good-looker,' said Mary, 'if you like 'em that way. I fancy the shirt. It's got class. And his hair. But he needs to get it cut right.'

'I'm going home.' Hal could stand no more. Her one idea had been not to see this creep Barry again. Yet here she was getting paired off with him.

Tim came after her. 'We're having a meeting as soon as it can be arranged. I'll get someone along from the Council. You like the idea? You're not against it?'

Hal turned to look at him. She was blushing, and for no good reason; she felt herself singled out.

'What does it matter what I think?'

'It seems – well, your friend Crimp gave me the idea that it does matter. That your lot won't come along without you.'

Hal found himself saying again: 'I don't know him. Well, not so's you could say *know*.' Fighting with a feller wasn't knowing him. 'He's got a cheek!' she muttered.

Without another word she turned away towards the canal, not waiting to see if Benjie was coming too. Above all not Betty and Mary.

Hal wanted no more explaining that night!

Six

HAL had made up her mind to tell Miss Camperdown about Barry. Not everything – not his name or where he lived – but she must talk to *someone*; and of all grown-ups Miss Camperdown was most to be trusted not to ask more questions than Hal wanted to answer.

Tuesday morning, hot, grey and airless, went by without an opportunity. First lesson was maths, which Hal was quite good at. But the class were put back to do kids' work because a group of Pakistanis, recently arrived in England, had joined the class. 'So,' as their elderly maths teacher crudely put it, 'we shall have to stick to something simple – something we can all understand even if we cannot talk English.' So they were set to wallpaper a room, after the maths mistress had drawn a diagram on the blackboard. Hal quickly drew her plans, finished her calculations and set herself to extricate Mary Malone sitting beside her, who had papered ceiling, windows and floor as well.

'Sure, but it was a lovely pattern, the wallpaper!' she sighed when the teacher came shunting up and down the rows like an old steam engine. Mary was ticked off for impertinence and when Hal protested that Mary was simply using her imagination *she* was ticked off, too.

As for the Pakistanis, who didn't have wallpaper at home, they remained dumb and totally mystified.

The next period was geography, which was fun for everyone, as Mr Springer was thoroughly in favour of Miss Camperdown's educational theories, so much so that he called a lesson a 'session', and soon had the rows of chairs and tables reorganized in suitably relaxed and untidy groups in which they worked among themselves and referred to him for guidance and inspiration. What they did was linked with their history project and Mr Springer, fired by the consciousness that in this way he was linked more closely with Miss Camperdown, darted from map to blackboard and flung over screens huge scrolls of his own invention, scrolls that rolled themselves up and had to be held down by willing hands. He was a small, light-footed American in a cool pale blue suit with a hot, flowered tangerine tie. Those of his class who understood the source of his enthusiasm, and approved of his fancying Miss Camperdown, followed his movements all the more intently as he drew diagrams of trade winds, listened as he described winds and waves, hot and copper skies, ocean currents, and brought vividly before their eyes what had hitherto been dry headings in textbooks: the unimaginable sufferings, the living death of slaves packed in a slave-ship.

Newcomers to the class who understood little, wanted to learn more. A boy from Kenya, seeing more in the drawings than he had understood from the talk, exclaimed that Arab dhows used just such a wind to bring carpets from Arabia to Mombasa. He described the long wait for the monsoon, the dhow with its curved lateen sail, how sometimes the voyage took too long, there was a plague, people died. His story took time, helped along by those who knew more English than he did; and Mr Springer forbore to point out that the Indian Ocean was not the Pacific. He only said, 'That's it.

That's the way it must've been. Waiting for a wind. Of course there were differences. The boats. Many things.'

'But it's what you were talking about,' Hal said, 'the winds and the currents?'

From there they got on to plants and fruit: the books called them 'products' of this and that country and had them cut down, squashed, dried, processed and packaged in a single deadening paragraph. Hal's group, the 'Lollards', had concentrated on plants and fruits growing on the African coast and on the islands across the Atlantic. Her father had got a book about Barbados from the library and to please him she had gone to some trouble to find out what plants with names like 'Tamarind' and 'Casuarina' looked like.

They were only names and pictures to her; but no sooner had she begun copying pictures on the blackboard than a clamour of recognition arose from the children who had come from countries where they grew. Each one wanted to draw his or her favourite fruit. The English children, Hal among them, listened enviously to a description of eating paw-paw for breakfast with a squeeze of fresh lime-juice; one boy showed how you bored holes in coconuts and poured its milk straight down your throat; another slashed an imaginary water-melon in quarters and mimed the juice running down his chin; an argument broke out as to how to cook mealies. Fruits you had to climb for, roots you dug for, fruit that brimmed with juice, crimson-fleshed, many-seeded, yellow oranges as big as grapefruit, a strange nut that hung from a scarlet apple – but the apple itself was poisonous. Tastes too strange to identify. Mangoes, now – how describe the flavour?

'Turpentine!' Mr Springer had just cried triumphantly

when the door opened and their English language teacher walked in. All but the newest arrivals were instantly silenced; the rest, meeting the full force of her steel-rimmed gaze, trailed away into dumbness.

'No doubt,' she addressed Mr Springer, 'the bell for break was inaudible?'

While Mr Springer rolled up his long unruly scrolls Miss Blunt stood like a sentry by her desk. Tables and chairs were restored to orderly rows, blackboards wiped clean, a number of children, hitherto too absorbed, discovered a pressing need to be excused. Miss Blunt was angry; but she was also triumphant, holding a watch in her hand. As the seconds ticked away Hal saw her half-smile, counting out poor Springy like a boxer floored. When at last he made for the door she cried, 'You realize of course that I shall have to keep them in during their free time before dinner?'

She was being cruel to Mr Springer because of Miss Camperdown, whose teaching methods, she had always maintained, would lead nowhere except to disorder and anarchy. And Mr Springer had just proved it.

'English language!' Hal muttered when at last the bell for dinner released them from a grind that was about as meaningless to them as to the Pakistanis. 'It's a total insult! Who do you think we are?'

Dinner was served in two sittings; and by the time Miss Blunt let them go and they had filed from one end of the huge building to the other they had missed the first sitting they were booked for and had to wait. Through glass doors Hal could see Miss Camperdown eating her pudding – there would be no chance to speak to her about Barry now. Leaning her head against the corridor wall Hal sighed: life was just too difficult!

'What's the matter?' Betty put a sympathetic arm round Hal's waist.

'Sure, she's in love!' Mary spoke teasingly and her eyes slid round with a look of curiosity. 'Who's the boyfriend? Tell us, Hal. The fair one – Barry – I could go for him.'

Betty's arm tightened. 'Don't be such a sap, Mary. That's all you think about – boyfriends!'

Hal shook herself free. There was an intensity about Betty's friendship which sometimes embarrassed her.

'Do me a favour!' she glared at them both. If they only knew what she'd got herself into! For how could she explain what had been going on, how the thing had started? All she had wanted was to be quit of Barry, be rid of the sick heavy feeling that nagged at her whenever she thought of him. *All* she wanted? She wanted to get him out of his house, to see him move when she told him to, to make him smile ... she wanted the thing kept secret, and not just for Barry's sake.

Hal looked down, frowning, at her feet; she scrumpled her toes like a little girl, overcome by conflicting feelings she did not understand.

'Come,' Mary persisted, ' 'tis a boy and she's been meeting him secretly and not telling us – you and your "homework"!'

The idea delighted Mary: a boyfriend was just what Hal needed, if only for reasons of prestige. 'Playing it cool and turning down dates is O.K. up to a point,' she nodded wisely, 'but you got to settle for a fella in the end – if only to go around with.'

Then a thought struck her: ' 'tis Crimp!' she cried, rolling her eyes and clutching her heart in mock despair. 'Crimp Watson!' she moaned.

Just then the refectory doors burst open and first dinners

came pouring through, bringing with them a smell of cooking that turned the waiting second dinners into ravening beasts. Behind Hal and the rest of her class riot threatened.

'Get aht of it!' someone shouted, 'you're not second dinners!'

Miss Camperdown, emerging, took in the situation. 'Stand aside, IVb.'

'We were kept in, miss!' cried Hal, as the rightful diners pushed past.

'I know.' Miss Camperdown's face was rigid, and Hal guessed she had heard all about Springy and Miss Blunt and was using every muscle not to come out with the violence she felt, seeing how *her* class had been treated.

'Greedy little beasts!' she let fly after the last boy in. Then she turned to IVb. 'I've seen to it,' she said, 'go on in.'

'You know why she was so mad?' Mary said as they queued up for their platefuls. 'Didn't you notice? Some of the lot that came out were old Blunt's class – second dinners, they are, sent in instead of us.'

'She must've kept us in on purpose!' Hal exclaimed. And Betty, wide-eyed at such wickedness: 'She must've fixed it. She must've meant all along to keep us in – before she found Springy'd made us late.'

'She reckoned he would,' Hal said as they sat down, elbowing one another for room. 'She had the whole thing worked out to catch Springy, the old cat!' The feud between Campers and her supporters and the Old Gang kept up an enjoyable tension that made school more than bearable.

But Hal, chewing on a piece of tough stewed steak, lost interest. She looked at Betty, picking at a vegetarian dish; Betty, whose dad worked at the B.B.C., who knew famous people and led what sounded like a fabulous life outside school. And Mary, shovelling down potatoes and gravy, who went to caffs and had grown-up boyfriends. Yet nothing seemed to interest them so much as what Springy had done and what Campers would do and how old Blunt . . .

'I've had enough!' she said, getting up abruptly, knocking Mary's elbow as she grabbed her half-filled plate.

'You're not ill?' Betty put out a solicitous hand.

'Oh – get lost!'

Betty looked hurt. Mary looked knowing, as Hal shovelled the contents of her plate into a bucket, was ticked off by a monitor for leaving so much, and pushed through the swing doors.

She found Miss Camperdown alone in their classroom, marking books and smoking. She did not look best pleased to see Hal.

'You're all to go out in the playground for half-an-hour,' she said.

Since Hal obstinately stood there she stubbed out her cigarette: her children were not to be encouraged to smoke, a rule she stuck to while actually teaching. Hal began to look along the shelves for a book.

'You heard!' Miss Camperdown said threateningly. 'You missed your lunch break, so you'll have to go out now.'

'Yes, miss.' Hal was unusually submissive.

'Well – go and let the others know. And don't come back.'

Hal went out into the corridor, meeting the first stragglers from lunch.

'We're to go out in the playground,' she said. The word was passed back. No one much wanted to go out; but the prospect of being seen outside when everyone else was inside, the row they'd purposely make, the questions that would arise, the way Campers would deal with the situation – everything that made them willing instruments of rebellion – such happy considerations sent them streaming joyously through glass-lined corridors, passing the message to other IVb's on their way.

Hal turned back to the classroom. She was set on talking to Miss Camperdown: she wanted the thing about Barry settled and off her mind. What was to happen to him? She wanted it fixed.

She turned the door handle carefully. Miss Camperdown had her feet up and had lit a fresh cigarette. Hal turned to the bookshelf and ran her hand over the books.

Miss Camperdown sat without moving. After a while she said, 'What's up?' Her mind was running on the morning's happenings, on Springy, the missed lunch-hour break ... Hal, most likely, had gone too far in rebellion. So she was not wholly surprised when Hal came over to her.

'How can a kid miss school?'

'You mean get sent away? Or stay away? No use trying it – I'd be round in no time to see your dad!'

'Not me,' Hal said, 'a boy. How can a kid miss school for weeks and weeks? In a room all day on his own. High up away from everyone. And no one know?'

'Is there a boy?'

Hal nodded.

'It can happen, or so I've heard. If people move, for instance.'

'That's it,' Hal interrupted, 'they moved – he came out of hospital and they moved.'

'There can be a time-lag. The old lot, the local education department, doesn't tell the new lot – the place where the child moves to. Or maybe they don't know he's moved, specially if he was in hospital. Finding out takes time.'

She looked inquiringly at Hal. 'This boy – he's a friend of yours?'

'No, not really. Couldn't be, I don't see how anyone could. He wouldn't let you.' She thought back to the time they'd had yesterday morning. How Barry had touched the grass and lain on his back and looked at the sky. And they had talked. She ran the palm of her hand over the back of a chair, gently, backwards and forwards. 'Maybe you could,' she said thoughtfully, 'be friends. Only not for long. He changes.'

Miss Camperdown looked covertly at her watch. 'What about his family?'

Hal related what Barry had told her about his mother. About his fear of other boys. 'He's scared to go out.'

'Oh *that,*' Miss Camperdown said reassuringly, 'not being able to go out, that's common enough. There's a name for it. And being scared of boys. Maybe he was bullied at school? One thing's certain, he needs help,' she concluded, stubbing out her cigarette. 'It sounds like a case for the Children's Officer, I'd say.'

'No!' cried Hal. 'No one's to know – that's why I told you. If we get in all them – the Welfare and that – he'd ... he'd ...'

'What? What d'you think he'd do?'

'He'd never speak to me again, that's for sure. And he'd be right.'

'D'you want him to?'

'I got him out,' said Hal fiercely, 'I made him!'

'He needs help,' Miss Camperdown said. 'More than you or I could give him.'

'*You* could.' Hal said.

'What do you want me to do?'

Hal knew now what she wanted – what would be right for Barry.

'Have him in your class, miss. In IVb. He'd be O.K. here, I know he would.'

'But you say he won't come out.'

'I'*d* get him here!' Hal said, her eyes blazing with sudden fury. 'Who does he think he is? If he got the chance of coming here . . .'

Miss Camperdown laughed. 'Barry's not the only one who "changes"! I can't make out if you like the kid or not. Enough to bother?'

Hal hunched her shoulders. 'He's on me mind.'

'The others'll be back in a minute.' Miss Camperdown tipped ash and stubs into a piece of paper, screwed it up and threw it in the wastepaper basket. 'Would you like me to come and see him?'

'Yeah. Yeah, I would!' Then her face clouded, 'But you can't. 'Cause he'd know I'd split on him.'

The sound of feet and voices filled the corridor outside.

'You say you can get him out. Get him to a caff or somewhere. We'll fix it later.'

IVb burst in, crowded round Miss Camperdown.

'We went in the playground like you said, miss,' the nearest boy cried breathlessly.

'Miss Blunt sent out to see what we were doing,' cried a girl.

'We told her we'd been sent!' It was a chorus.

'Then Miss Blunt came out herself – told us we were –' Miss Blunt's words were drowned in happy chanting.

'Shut up!' Miss Camperdown stood up, and they could see, not hear her words. Silence, more or less, followed.

'So,' she said, 'you missed recreation. So – you were sent out. But did anyone tell you to behave like stupid hooligans?' Her voice rose to a shout. 'Groups now,' she said in her ordinary voice, 'and double quick about it.'

Lollards, Levellers and Luddites collected together in their allotted corners, put up screens like portable notice-boards, got out their books and pictures and maps.

'Boring isn't it?' Campers' look of distaste, as she surveyed her class, referred to Miss Blunt and her allies, not to themselves. 'Dead boring. For you as for me. But that's the way things are, the way the world is, you may as well get used to it. *Irrelevant!* Irrelevant,' she repeated flatly, scrabbling through her bag, from habit, to find a cigarette, looking at the packet and putting it away unopened. 'And now – let's not waste any more time.'

'That'll not be the end of it!' Mary Malone whispered, looking over Hal's shoulder at a map.

As she spoke a senior girl knocked, entered, handed Miss Camperdown a note and went out again.

'It'll be from the Head!' Betty whispered.

'He won't get much change out of Campers!'

'The Head's on Campers' side anyway. Remember what he said last Open Day?'

Hal, who had been pinning up a drawing on the hessian-covered screen, looked round. 'Turn it off!' she said, using Miss Camperdown's special bored voice. 'Didn't you hear her say? It's *irrelevant!*'

Half an hour before school ended, Hal went up to Campers: 'Can I go early, please, miss?'

Campers sized the girl up, her eager, anxious look. 'If it's really important,' she said, 'and since you haven't tried anything on – no lies – O.K. But don't make it a habit.'

Hal fled. She made straight for the site. If Campers would take Barry on, he'd be off her mind. How to bring them together? She hadn't worked that one out by the time she stood on the site opposite Barry's window. Would he look out? Soon kids would be pouring over the place.

At last she saw him. He signed that he was coming down. She heard the door open, the box being dragged up to the wall. Then Barry himself, head and shoulders, his thin face sharpened with uncertainty. Then (and once more Hal felt that heady sense of power) he smiled.

'Come on down,' she said. He hesitated, looked both ways – Then, from the Institute end, two or three boys appeared.

'I can't,' he said.

Hal jumped the ditch between the grass and the wall, grasped the top of the wall, swung herself up and astride.

'Why not?' Her face was close to his.

Barry shrugged: 'You know why'.

'You came over before – when there was lots of kids.'

He had, too. Hadn't stopped to think about his fears. But then Hal had needed him – or so he'd thought; for he had been certain Hal wouldn't support the idea of the playground, of the place being spoiled. But he'd been wrong. And what was the use of explaining?

'Well, I can't now,' was all he would say.

'You let them help you get back over the wall.'

He said nothing. At the time, he hadn't minded. But he wasn't coming out now, though there was no point in saying so again.

'Look,' said Hal, 'It's the boys you mind, isn't it? You're scared they're going to knock you around?'

As he said nothing, she went on, 'Come out with me. Not now. When there are no kids around. You say you don't mind going out with your mum. Come out with me. We could walk by the canal.' Barry's face tightened.

'Try,' she urged him, 'just try. You can't stay up there. Anything could happen. They'll find out – the Welfare and all. They'll make you.'

She put her hands over his wrists. 'Try. Only you'll have to come out yourself. Not this way. People would see us. And I'm not coming to your house.'

There was to be no explaining – no talk with his mother – Hal had already decided she would hate his mum, somehow it must be all her fault. 'You get to the paper shop at the corner near your street around six, and I'll be there. Next Saturday.'

Any minute now Mary and the lot of them would be coming through the gap. And she'd got to get home. Explain why she'd missed tea, not changed her school clothes. Hal dropped down, giving him one backward look.

Barry stayed on the wall. Hal made anything seem possible. Then he dropped back, shaking all over.

Seven

WHEN Saturday came, Barry got his mother to cut and wash his hair.

'You're taking more of an interest,' she said approvingly, 'playing your record-player. And them paperbacks we bought at the second-hand stall this morning. Try to take an interest, that's what they said at the hospital.' You'll soon be well enough to go to school, she would have liked to add. But did not dare.

As soon as they had had supper she said: 'You won't be wanting to come out again? You'll be tired after this morning?'

Barry knew she wanted to go out on her own. She had washed and changed into her smartest outfit before supper. 'You go off,' he said, anxious on his own account. Hal wouldn't wait. 'I'll wash up,' he offered, as she went into the other room for her handbag. This unusual courtesy had her back in an instant, full of guilty affection. 'You're sure?' she asked. 'You'll be all right on your own?'

With her face close to his Barry could see how deeply she longed for him to say yes. There must be something up, he thought, something quite special, but was too intent on his own affairs to wonder what. He put both arms round her in a way which reassured her, but which he was beginning to feel too old for.

'Be good, son!' she said as she always did, and in an instant had swept up her white bag and was gone.

Barry listened to her clip-clopping down the stairs, waiting to hear the front door slam; for she had a way of returning to see if he was all right. Then he dragged his shirt over his head, dashed water into the washing-up bowl, scrubbed his face, neck and arms, dived into a toffee-coloured, polo-necked sweatshirt, zipped himself into hip-hugging bell-bottomed sky-blue pants, made for the stairs, came back for money, which he took from a jar on his mother's mantel shelf, and his latch-key, back again down the stairs . . . At the bottom he remembered the boys outside.

For a second he stood there fighting down nausea, trying to breathe. He thought of Hal at the corner. He got the door open.

The street was empty, at least of children. He crossed the road, turned out of Bute Street and there, at the next crossing, was Hal, standing by the newsagent's as she had arranged to do!

'Been here long?' he panted, coming up to her.

She shook her head. She was wearing the same orange pink shirt he remembered her in the morning she had come to the site on her own, and a skirt that matched the orange. Her hair was tied up with pink ribbon.

'It was me mum,' he said, 'she was late getting out.'

'You said she might be.'

It was enough for Hal that Barry had come; she had known all along that he might not. At first sight of him relief, triumph, and a heady sense of power flooded her with warmth; she smiled.

Barry could not smile back; he tried, but his lips only

stretched and tightened; there was a lump in his chest, in his throat. Seeing her was such painful happiness.

'How about a walk?' she suggested. 'We could go down along the towpath.'

Instinctively, as though to guard against his turning for home, she held out her hand. When Barry took it he felt safe, as one of her sisters might have done, or so she sensed. Their way took them past the market. The crowds, the noise, even the fact that the pub his mother frequented was at the further end of the street – nothing meant much to Barry beside the reality of Hal as she walked a little in front of him, lingering by the fruit stalls, holding her hand behind her with upturned fingers into which Barry's fingers fitted. 'Aren't they lovely?' she said, turning her head, nodding towards a pile of huge green watermelons, some cut to show their rosy flesh and black seeds.

'The colour of your hair-ribbon,' Barry said. 'Would you like one?' He put his other hand on his hip-pocket where the money was.

She laughed and shook her head. 'The juice,' she laughed, 'it'd run all over us!'

The more exotic the fruit, the longer she stayed to look at it. Because people from so many different countries lived near by there were many fruits and vegetables that were strange to Barry, green, purple, orange, yellow. They came to a stall which was partly cleared.

'Mangoes!' the barrow-boy shouted, 'ripe mangoes – come on ladies, two for twenty to clear, two for 20p!'

'Mangoes!' Hal turned to him with shining eyes, 'Did you hear?'

'If you'd like some?'

They stood in a queue behind a woman, darker-skinned

than Hal, but with the same satiny bloom on her round arms. She was swathed in orange and purple with a gauze scarf tied over her high-piled hair.

She held out a bag and the man filled it.

'Two,' Barry said when their turn came, hoping two would be enough.

As they walked away from the market Barry asked if Hal often ate mangoes?

'First time.'

'How d'you know what they'll taste like?'

'I want to find out. Springy says they taste of turpentine.'

Hal began to tell Barry about school, about Springy and the history comp and the argument they'd had about mangoes and how the unspeakable Miss Blunt had interrupted them.

'My school wasn't like that!' Barry marvelled.

They had come out on the towing-path in a different place from the Bute Street Site; at Hal's suggestion they sat down on the grass verge to eat the mangoes.

'Springy was right,' Hal spluttered, holding her hand under her chin to catch the juice. 'Turpentine!'

'It's got such a lot of tastes,' Barry said, 'some at the front of your tongue and some at the back.'

'And some more after you've swallowed it.'

'You don't get much for your money,' Barry held the big stone between thumb and finger, 'did you really like it?'

'Mm!' She leant back, supported by her arms, her head tipped back. Barry, too, gazed up into the sky, a pure, warm blue now that the sun had gone from it. On the opposite bank were houses that had been neglected but were being painted up, with wild overgrown gardens that reached to the water's edge. Here and there lamps were lit; glass doors stood open;

from one house came the sound of voices and laughter, and a smell of cooking reached across the still waters. A pleasure-boat passed, heralded by a man with a microphone, swishing the water into waves that went on lapping afterwards in the stillness, cooling the air and stirring up smells of mud and water-weed and the green algae that slimed the bricks.

A water-rat plopped into the canal.

'There's another!' Barry made to chuck his mango stone at it, but Hal stopped him.

'Bury it,' she said. 'Let's bury them both.'

They tore away the turf and pressed the stones close together in shallow holes and put the turf back. Barry laid his hand on the place where they were hidden and looked at Hal.

'They will never grow up,' he said.

'You've got eyes like cat's eyes,' she said. His eyes had a way of narrowing almost to slits, with creases at the corners that turned up. 'They look better than when I first saw you. They were red round the edges.' Hal was remembering what Mary had remarked – that Barry was a good-looker.

She would have liked Mary to see him now. His hair, cut just short of shoulder-length, was pale yellow, fine and silky.

'Bin watching you all week,' he said.

'Don't like being watched.'

'Not just you – the whole lot of you. You bin tearing the site up. Where'd you get them pick-axes and spades from?'

'The Council, I s'pose. They came –'

'I saw them come. In a truck with a load of old wood and poles and planks.'

'The Institute people let them through. There's that bit of ground they don't use. They're going to have gardens there, anyone who wants to – and animals – budgies, rabbits. And a safe place for young kids.'

The last few days had been as absorbing, as agonizing for Barry as any during the time of the Game. At first the children had spent most of their time arguing in groups. Sometimes the whole lot – and more came every day – would crowd round the bloke from the Institute. Then they would break away, seemingly at random, like streams eddying over flooded ground. A boy would pace out a distance, another write down measurements on a clip-board. Every day there was more to do. The younger children bore away the planks and began to build them, mostly lean-to houses round the old brick ventilator. The older ones, Hal among them, were occupied in clearing the scrub round Crimp Watson's old hide-out. It was these spades and mattocks and picks that fascinated and repelled Barry; they were grown-up tools, heavy to swing, yet boys like Crimp could use them; they were tools for destruction. With these weapons every green bush and plant in the place could be torn up. Every day he watched Hal to see what she would do, how far she would let them go. Yet she behaved like the rest, hacking away at roots and exulting when a particularly old tusk was wrenched from the earth!

By Friday evening the clearing round Crimp's hill was finished. One side of it was revealed as a bare slope overhung by a bough of the tree that had been his 'look-out'. A rope had been slung over the bough and knotted.

'I saw you swing out on that rope,' Barry said, musing on the remembered scene.

'Yeah. Swinging off into space – it's like flying.' She looked at him. 'You should've come out, you really should.'

'I almost did.'

'Your trouble is you think people are looking at you. Well, they're not. No one would notice you. It'd be just the same

. . .' At school, she had been going to say. But this was not the moment. Hal was recalled to the chief object of the evening, the reason why they were here now. Miss Camperdown and the caff.

'I could do with a coffee.' She got up. Again, she held out her hand.

Unwillingly Barry joined her. 'I'd have liked to stay here a bit.'

The last of the sun still reddened the chimney-pots of the tall houses opposite. But shadows in the gardens deepened; people who had come to sit out there spoke in low voices; a cigarette glowed. Once or twice as Barry and Hal sat by the towpath, couples had passed by.

'Couldn't we stay a bit? It's quiet here.' Barry pressed his toe into the turf which concealed their mango stones.

'We can come back if you want,' she said, with her eye on his foot. She turned away, inwardly impatient: Miss Camperdown might have arrived at the caff by now. Barry went after her, drawn by her cool fingers along the path, down an alley that led to a shopping street where he hesitated.

Hal let go his hand and for a moment was lost among the passers-by. Barry panicked, quickened his pace, caught up with her and was relieved when she turned into a doorway. From within came the muffled thud of drums.

Inside the caff it was too dark to see much. Hal made her way to a corner where there were vacant seats under a red glass lamp. Barry slid along the bench beside her.

She said with a touch of anxiety, 'I s'pose you got some money left?'

Barry patted his hip pocket.

Hal waited, then, when he didn't offer, she suggested,

'Shall I get the coffees, then?' Hal was now on tenterhooks; she couldn't see Miss Camperdown, but she might be in any of the angles and nooks; or she might not have come. Worst of all, she might have got here and gone away again.

'I don't mind.'

'Give us the money, then.' Some boyfriend! thought Hal, imagining Mary's comments. When she saw the money she said: 'We could have cakes.'

'All right.'

'You don't want to choose?'

He shook his head. He made no attempt to help her when she came back with two glass cups and saucers.

'I've just seen someone I know.' Her voice was unnaturally high-pitched. 'D'you mind if I ask her over?'

To her surprise he made no objection. She went back to the counter for the cakes, then left him for a part of the caff he couldn't see. Barry instantly felt scared. He took an incautious sip of scalding hot coffee, knowing well enough that his fear – of her walking out on him – was unreal. Yet so was everything around him.

At first, seeing the girl who came up behind Hal, carrying a half-empty cup, Barry thought she was a school-friend, dressed more or less like Hal herself. But when she sat down and spoke he saw she was a good deal older.

'Hullo,' she greeted him. 'I won't, thanks,' she answered Hal, who, still holding Barry's change, was offering to buy her a cake.

Breaking a silence Miss Camperdown said, 'It's nice and quiet here. The music's never so loud you can't hear yourself speak.'

'It's jazz,' Barry said.

'You like jazz? So did my boyfriend. That's why we used

to come here. Stan – the manager – records his own tapes.'

Hal wondered why they didn't come here any more. There was a recognizable hardness in Campers' voice, and Hal, remembering her saying her boyfriend worked at the Institute, wondered if they'd broken up.

'Barry's got a tape-recorder,' she said, 'his mum bought it for him when he come out of hospital.'

'Who are your favourite musicians, groups or whatever?'

'No one special.' Then, because his answer seemed rude, he went on, 'I don't remember names so good since I was ill.' In fact, he knew almost nothing about jazz; neither did Campers. So conversation died once more.

'Oh, miss!' Hal suddenly relaxed. 'We had mangoes! They were selling them off in the market and Barry bought two and we ate them down by the canal.'

'I've only had them once. They've got a queer taste.'

'Springy – Mr Springer said they tasted of turpentine. They do too. But that's only one taste – there are so many, all in one fruit!'

'I think I will have another cup – no, don't get up. I want some cigs too.'

When she left Barry whispered. 'You called her "miss".'

'Did I?' Hal spoke nervously. She and Campers had agreed that Miss Camperdown's identity had better not be disclosed at this first meeting, if it could be avoided.

'You're not saying she's your *teacher!*' Barry was eyeing Miss Camperdown's mini-skirt, taking in her general appearance, so unlike any teacher he'd ever come across.

'Yeah.' Hal sat with her hands squeezed between her knees. It had suddenly become enormously important that Barry should come to her school, above all that he should never guess that she and Campers had plotted this meeting.

On Campers' return, Hal said helplessly, 'He asked if you were my teacher.'

'Oh.' Campers, equally nonplussed, stirred her coffee. Then, deliberately, she began to talk to Hal about school, asking how Benjie was getting on during his first year, and about Mary's mum who had been in hospital. They talked about the history comp and how it was timed to be held the next Parents' Day. Hal began to tell her about Miss Blunt and Mr Springer but Campers stopped her, saying grimly, 'I heard.'

It wasn't so much what they said as the way they talked that held Barry's attention: they talked as equals. He couldn't fit Miss Camperdown into any school of his imagining.

Before long Hal's teacher said, 'I've got to go. Can I give you two a lift?'

'Could you?' Hal glanced at Barry. 'We walked quite a way.'

Miss Camperdown, who had already noticed Barry's exhausted face, led the way out of the caff, calling 'Goodnight!' to the proprietor, who seemed to know her well.

Miss Camperdown's car was parked round the corner. Barry was afraid he would never walk the short distance, but to cover his anxiety he said casually to Hal, 'That wasn't a bad caff.'

'I never bin there before,' she said. 'Mary – my friend you met – she told me about it.'

'I wouldn't mind going again.'

'Yeah?' He was not too tired to notice Hal's surprise and pleasure.

In the car he thought, that teacher never asked me where I go to school. He asked to be put down by the newsagent's at the corner.

Hal, who had been sitting behind, got out too so as to sit in front with Miss Camperdown. 'It's late, isn't it?' he heard her say to Hal. 'I'd better come home with you. Else your dad'll go for you.'

'Could you, miss? They won't mind if they know I've been with you.'

Barry waited till they had driven away before walking the distance to his own door. And, after all, he wasn't as wobbly as he had expected to be. His mother's light was on and as he crossed the street she threw up her window.

Before he reached the front door she had opened it.

'Where on earth you bin?'

Quickly reasoning that she wouldn't have been back long herself and couldn't know how long he'd been away, Barry answered, 'Where *you* bin?'

She didn't reply, but passed him and went up the stairs, softly, for she had changed into slippers.

Upstairs, he flung himself down on his bed and lay with his hands behind his head.

'You never did the washing-up!' she grumbled mildly. Then she looked at him curiously. 'You got your new tee-shirt on.'

Barry continued to stare at the ceiling.

'Sunday tomorrow,' his mother remarked, 'we're going over to see your auntie. Mr Barnes is coming. Remember him? The manager of the Co-op?'

'O.K.,' he agreed abstractedly, recalling Mr Barnes. Bald-headed. Gave his mum endless credit, like he told Hal. And a box of stuff at Christmas. 'Don't mind if I do.'

'That's a nice change I must say!' But she didn't sound altogether pleased; she had expected a fight, and not having one was deflating.

Eight

SOME days later, Barry slowly climbed the stairs. He had spent all day in the playground, a whole June day, beginning by helping Tim and the men who had been got in by the Council to make the big hut which was to be for wet days, and have toilets. The rest of the playground was to be made by the children themselves, whatever way they wanted it to be.

Tim took an interest in Barry: 'Shouldn't lie around too much,' he said. 'Rest, yes, when you feel tired. But there's plenty to do. Strengthen your muscles.' Tim seemed to know all about Barry's recent illness. 'There's nothing much wrong with you now. The more you get out and about the better.'

'You a doctor?' Barry asked him.

'No. But I know something about viral infections – that's what you've had. That was part of my research job.' He jerked his head towards the Bute Institute. Barry gathered Tim had had to stop working there because the money for the research ran out. But Tim didn't encourage questions about his work. He was bitter, Barry could see that, and small wonder, having to stop for want of cash.

Barry sometimes felt that he was a little bit of work left over, something Tim could finish and make a good job of, the same as he was determined to do with the playground. But Tim's detachment suited Barry.

Benjie and Kevin had made holes in Barry's wall and fixed a rope up to make climbing it easier for him. At first he had retreated when the site filled up after school; but soon he stayed on till supper time.

Hal and the others from Jefferson School were friendly, but left him alone, to help clear the site if he wanted to, or go off and lie around, in one of the places that were to be left wild. Hal's kid sisters used to trail around after him, Barry liked this, at first because he knew that in this way Hal was left free. Then for their own sakes.

Hal spoke of them always as though they were one thing: 'Anderandbell.' But Barry soon saw they were two, with very different characters, Anda strong-minded, resilient, living from day to day, not minding the hard times. Like Hal, thought Barry. Bell was no more than a baby, soft, needing a hand, often with a puzzled, lost look, used to being left behind.

This June evening, then, when Barry was climbing his dark stairs, his head was full of the day, the light, the leaves, the sound of voices. One cheek was burning. For he had slept a long time, and the sun had crept round. Bell and Anda had wakened him, plumping themselves down on his chest, smelling of soap, noisily affectionate.

'You hid!' cried Anda.

'Hid!' echoed Bell.

'We nearly had to go home and leave you.'

'Gosh!' exclaimed Barry, 'it *is* late!'

He hadn't been home to dinner: Tim had shared his bread and cheese, and beer. Barry didn't much like beer, but he liked being asked to share. Same with the men on the site. If one offered him a fag he took it, but never half-smoked it. All the time he was feeling stronger, surer, less of a kid.

So, deliberately, he stayed out, knowing his mother would have brought back food at mid-day, waited in vain, and returned to work. A coolness had arisen, a distance had widened between them. Most nights Mrs Padgitt went out after preparing his supper. Never said where she was going. But once he heard her tell a neighbour she'd been 'up West'.

Quite often Barry went back to the site where, these light evenings, there was plenty going on. But he had never before stayed out all day.

So now he was climbing slowly, foreseeing his mother's complaining voice, the spoilt food.

But his mother seemed unlike herself, uneasy, and only called hesitantly, 'So you're back, then?'

'Bin out in the playground – the site.'

Mrs Padgitt came through; she had washed and changed into a dress Barry had never seen, close-fitting, made of shiny stuff. 'Mrs Roebuck's been here. She came early and you were late, so she had her fitting.'

She took two chicken dinners out of the small oven, each a complete meal covered in silver foil, and dished them on to plates, sprouts, mashed and fried potatoes, bread sauce and gravy. Barry's favourite food.

'You might've come in at mid-day – I've had these heated through twice.'

'Sorry. I was down on the site. Had something to eat there.'

'I saw you. That dark feller with a foxy beard – he runs the place?'

Barry was astonished. 'How did you know?'

His mother looked pleased at having impressed him. 'I know more than you think!'

She waited for Barry to question her further. But Barry's

thoughts were in turmoil: how much did she know? About Hal? About the walk they'd had? The caff?

'Oh, yes,' his mother purred, 'I know all about the adventure playground. Mrs Roebuck's on the committee. She was there Saturday. They were all there, people from the Council, the Mayor . . . You must've seen her.'

'I shouldn't know her if I did.' Barry was reminding his mother that he had only heard about her best customer, never been allowed to see her. 'Anyhow, I wasn't down there Saturday.'

'She favours the idea, Mrs Roebuck does. Thinks there's a lot in these adventure playgrounds. Good for you, she says!'

'I didn't know she knew about me?'

It was his mother's turn to look evasive. 'As you well know, I've not told people about you being here. Not since we moved. Because of your being too ill. Not wanting to go to school. I didn't know how to explain.'

'But you have now?'

Mrs Padgitt got up, cleared away their plates and produced two 'Royal Chocolate Whirls', a party sweet bought off the ice-cream man.

'Melted a bit,' she said apologetically. 'I had to put them on my window-sill when you didn't come in.'

'But you have now,' Barry persisted, 'told Mrs Roebuck?'

'I had to. She wanted to come through and see the site from your window. Besides . . . It's no use, son. Somebody had to know. I don't know why the Welfare, or the school officer, or whoever it is, hasn't bin round before. It's only on account of you that I've kept silent. I could be took up for this. Mrs Roebuck said so. Not telling about you. But if they come she says she can make things all right. Explain about your illness. She's got ideas for you. Wait till you hear ... there's a school she knows about.'

Barry sat silent, staring at the confection on his plate.

'Eat up, do. Here, have my cherry as well.'

When he didn't respond she rushed on. 'You don't have to go now. Not till you're really better. But – oh, it's a wonderful chance, Barry – just wait till I show you!' She went next door and returned with a glossy prospectus. 'You could start right away if you was well enough. At this school. Mrs Roebuck says you'd soon get strong there, in the country, with proper exercise. Mr Roebuck is one of the governors. And think of it, son – everything found and not a penny to pay! Because I'm in the trade.'

Pushing aside Barry's plate she opened the school prospectus at a double-page spread. Rows and rows of boys, big boys seated with their arms folded, little ones cross-legged at their feet. In the background a huge building with a portico and pillars like a church.

'There's everything. A swimming pool, a chapel – proper public school, Cranmere College.'

'How did you get this?'

'Mrs Roebuck. She's ready to see to everything.'

'If she brought it she must've known about me before. You said today was the first time. You bin planning this.'

He was on his feet, conscious that he was taller, and probably stronger than his mother.

'I had to tell someone,' she complained. 'You never think what it's like for me. No one to turn to, not to know what to do for the best. You never think of anyone but yourself.'

Barry got up and looked out of the window. There were fewer children on the site, but still plenty going on.

'I'm not going,' he said, his hands clenched, thrust down inside the band of his jeans.

She came up behind him and put her arm round his neck.

Violently he shook himself free. 'You can't make me!' But he was afraid she could. She and Mrs Roebuck.

'Anyhow,' he burst out, 'I'm going to school at half-term. It's all fixed.' Maybe Hal could fix it. Or that teacher at the caff.

'What did you say?' In her astonishment she pulled him round to face her.

'I bin planning things too.' His face was white, his lips pale and tight.

'You can't've. Who've you been talking to? What school, anyway?'

'I – can't remember the name. One near here. Not too far anyway.'

'What've you been up to? I've not seen no headmaster. You can't've seen him on your own. It's not true.' She looked at him searchingly. His face told her nothing. She took up the school prospectus as though to persuade him. He snatched it away and tried to tear it; but the thick, expensive paper was hard to tear. He flung it at her.

'I'm going out!' he cried.

She did not try to stop him.

Nine

THE first person he saw when he climbed over the wall was Mary Malone.

'Hya!' she greeted him.

'Has everyone gone home?'

'They're up the other end,' she indicated the newly erected hut. 'And if you're going that way,' she called after him, 'tell Crimp Watson I'm not waiting for him.'

Barry nodded distractedly. 'Oh,' she called again, 'and if it's Hal you're looking for you won't find her there.'

He turned back.

'There's no need to look like that!' she laughed. 'You fancy her, don't you? But the way you're looking now, boy, no one'll fancy *you!*'

'I gotta find her.' Barry's fear was that she might have gone home, miles away probably, and he wasn't going to ask this girl where she lived.

'She's in there,' Mary obligingly directed him to the largest tunnel entrance to Hal's former hideout. 'It's being bull-dozed, part of it, to make football pitches, and she went to fetch something.'

This was not how Barry had planned to enter the jungle. It was for Hal to take him, to make him free of her jungle. The scene had so often been re-enacted in his imagination.

But now he had to find her wherever she was.

He dived into the tunnel, bent double, unconscious of

exhaustion, not caring that he was whipped and scratched. There was not much light and he had no idea of his direction. But where there was a fork he chose the track that seemed most worn. Once or twice he chose wrong and came to a dead end. There were openings off the main track, bays sometimes floored with newspaper as though people had lain there. There were bad smells, not just of urine or excrement but of vomit; and smells he could not recognize. The jungle was not as he had imagined it. Mostly the tunnel ran through privet and some spade-leaved bush, and this was not so bad. Hawthorn and blackthorn thickets were the worst. All the time he was climbing slightly, with the slope of the site; sometimes he fell into sandy tunnels, sometimes into pools of stagnant water. He did not expect to find Hal at once, for from watching at his window he knew the paths twisted and penetrated most of the bushy area.

Hal! he wanted to shout; for she might be leaving by some other way, might even now be gone. Panic grew as light faded. Hal! he cried soundlessly; for though his pride was soon lost, his fear of her anger at hearing her name shouted, at knowing others might hear, was greater than his panic. Once or twice he stopped to listen, lest she should be moving close to him. But there was no sound except the hiss of leaves above his head; a wind had got up.

At last he collapsed in a small clearing bare of grass. He was finished. He would stay here all night. He would not go home. He would *not* go home.

It was here that Hal found him, lying on his face.

She let out a little cry; the suddenness, the unexpectedness, and then the stillness of his body shocked her.

Before she could speak Barry blurted out: 'You gotta help me, I can't go home – me mum – a school . . .'

He was too breathless to be coherent. Hal waited. Then she said, 'I've gotta go.' But she stayed there, kneeling beside him, a rusty tin box under one arm: 'Can't help if you don't tell me.'

He turned over on his back and put his arms behind his head, staring up into the interlaced branches.

'I want to come to your school.'

'Thought you didn't want to go to school?' Hal had had a talk with Miss Camperdown. They had gone over the problem of getting Barry out of the house, of approaching his mother, of the many obstacles that must be overcome before Barry could be got to school. It was unrealistic, Miss Camperdown had concluded. Hal had better give up the idea. She herself would do nothing, because she had promised in advance not to tell anyone. Sooner or later the boy would be discovered; the sooner the better. Maybe then something could be done to get him into the Jefferson.

And here was Barry *asking* if he could come!

'They've found out?' she asked. 'The school officer? The Welfare?'

Barry shook his head. Calmer now, he told her about Mrs Roebuck, about the school prospectus, the chapel, the big boys sitting with crossed arms, the blazer and tie, the pants and socks: 'All found, me mum says. You can see why she's dead keen. Not a penny to pay. And a posh school. She wants to get quit of me.'

'Yeah,' Hal nodded. She could see why anyone might want to get quit of Barry. But his mum! 'I can't see our mum sending us away. Not however much we got on her wick.'

'I told her it was fixed for me to come to your school. At half-term.'

Barry turned his head to see how she took this.

Hal let out a sigh. 'Miss Camperdown might fix it.' She sighed with relief, because after all, what Barry wanted was so easy. At first his wild talk had scared her – he might come out with anything. But she sighed, too, because, if Miss Camperdown *did* fix it, she'd really have Barry on her back for keeps, a thought which, at the moment, turned her up.

'I dunno,' she murmured, bewildered by her own changeable feelings. She put the box down. She stretched herself out beside him, and lay propped up on her arms, looking at him.

From the moment of Hal's saying Miss Camperdown might fix it, his anxieties vanished. Colour returned to his face, the cat-like creases at the corners of his eyes disappeared and his thin lips relaxed and curved.

'What about the boys?' she reminded him. 'You know – the boys in your street you were afraid of. There's lots of boys at school. Big ones: they might go for you.'

'I shan't mind.' He might have added: As long as I'm with you nothing frightens me. But he sensed that such a remark would irritate her. Once at her school Barry imagined that she would be constantly in his sight, and the thought made him smile, fleetingly.

'You look better when you smile,' she said. She searched his face to see what Mary Malone had meant when she called him a good-looker. 'I could fancy him,' Mary had said.

'I don't feel like smiling often,' Barry replied. 'It's an effort to smile when you don't feel like it.'

'You're all right when you're serious.'

'Serious?'

'Like now.'

Hal put a finger on his forehead and traced a line down

his nose and round the lines about his mouth, which was no longer thin and stretched; his lips, relaxed, had filled out.

'You frown so much,' she said.

'I'm not frowning now,' he said huskily.

He couldn't see all the details of her face, with her head against the fading light that filtered through the leaves. But he knew her features by heart. He would have liked to put up his hand to touch her face, her fine dark eyebrows, her nose, the beads of sweat on her upper lip. But the feeling aroused in him by her touching him was so new, so overwhelming, that he dared not move.

'We should go.' Her face was so close he could feel her breath on his cheek.

'You came to fetch your treasure?' He must say something – anything – to keep her there.

She drew away: 'I don't get you?'

'The box.'

'You round the twist?' she laughed, but not unkindly. 'They're going to bulldoze the bushes round here – not all of it, but enough to make two football pitches. Crimp's dad's lending us his bulldozer. He comes along and works it in the evenings. So I came to fetch the tin.'

'Can't stand him.'

'Crimp? He turns me up too. But there are things he's good at – he's strong.'

'The tin – what's in it? Or don't you want to say?'

'Why not? The things you come out with! There's some old stuff in it, playing cards and that, Anda and Bell's bits and pieces.'

'Is that all?'

'Well, not quite all. There's some fags.'

'Is that what you did? Smoked!'

'Sometimes.'

'When you took prisoners what did you do with them?'

'Nothing much. It was kid's stuff, the Game. Kid's stuff. I told you. Why d'you keep on about it?'

'It started as a kid's game. Then it changed. You said so. I saw you. The fighting – that changed.'

Hal was silent. If he didn't know what went on there was no way of telling him even if she had wanted to.

No words to describe the games they played, the fights that continued. Truly, as Hal had said, it was a kid's game which she and her friends were too old to be playing.

For one thing was certain about Barry: you couldn't ask him to play games. This was what Hal had meant when she said he was serious. Yet in other ways he was childlike.

'Treasure!' she mocked him, but gently. 'You and your jungle. Some jungle!'

'It's a bit of a mess when you get into it.'

'The meths drinkers used to come till they were turned out, Fred said.'

'Fred?' Barry was instantly jealous at this new name.

'He's a helper Tim's got. Got snakes round his arms – tattooed. Used to be a sailor.'

'Couples still get in at night,' Barry said. 'But I s'pose it won't be so easy for them now they've closed the gaps up and made a proper gate.'

For some time now sounds had reached them: indeterminate murmurs lower than the hissing leaves in the wind overhead, a girl's laughter quickly stifled. These sounds seemed far away, and served only to increase their sense of being alone secretly, peacefully together. For there was something peaceful about Barry, about his stillness and attentiveness. If she made a world of security for Barry simply by being there, it was also true that he, as he was now, offered Hal, pressed upon and pulled apart by the currents in her full life, a place to be, a quiet place.

She lay close to him, looking at his face, a whitish glimmer.

'Look – we must go.'

Barry sat up. 'Will you go ahead?'

'I'm not coming. I'll get out another way.' Hal had recognized the far-off laughter; it was Mary Malone's voice. She didn't want to be seen with Barry. Why should she mind? Somehow she did. 'You'll find the way?'

When Barry hesitated she said: 'I'll go ahead. But I'm not coming out with you.'

Ten

DURING the days that followed Barry waited in agonizing uncertainty to see if Hal had been able to get her teacher to 'fix things' so that he could come to her school. Hal herself had not come to the playground. Benjie had told him why. 'Dad won't let her. She didn't do her homework. And then she stayed out late, like she did once before. Said he'd belt her if she did it again. He didn't belt her. But he made her stop in.'

'She didn't say anything – about my coming to your school?'

Benjie shook his head.

Barry spent most of his time on the site, rather than lying around in his room waiting for news. He lay around when it was fine, and sometimes Tim offered him jobs to do, like sorting a heap of old bricks and knocking the mortar off, which soon tired him, though the children who came after school went at the work enthusiastically. They liked doing real things, as opposed to just playing. The second morning Tim took him swimming at the local baths, and he got through the whole afternoon sleeping it off. But there was the evening to come, to wait through.

His mother said nothing more about the boarding school. This silence was so unlike her that Barry was afraid she was doing some fixing on her own, and that she would suddenly have him clothed in the free uniform that had so taken her fancy, and whip him off to the school without warning.

They addressed one another with a new, wary politeness. Barry felt his mother's eye on him all the time he was with her; clearly she could not make out his unusual behaviour. Once she tried embracing him in the old way, but Barry quickly withdrew.

'What's the matter, son?' Barry could see that she really minded his coldness, was not only puzzled but hurt.

'Don't know what you mean,' he said evasively.

'I don't know what's come over you. Ever since you come out of hospital it was Mum this and Mum that, don't leave me, can't go out on me own, won't see a doctor, won't go to school – you've had me up the wall not knowing what's for the best, and them saying in hospital that you had to be kept interested, had me up the wall, you did. And now ...'

'Maybe I'm better?'

'We used to be so close.' She came towards him again.

'It's nothing, Mum, really it isn't.' He gave her a peck on the cheek.

She gave him one of her searching, sly looks that turned him up.

'You haven't been hearing anything? – no one's been saying things?'

Instantly Barry's mind flashed to the blazer, the purple and orange tie.

'Heard what?' He could hardly get the words out. 'I'm not going,' he croaked, 'you can't make me – I'll run away sooner.'

'Sooner than what?'

'Go to that school you bin planning.'

'*That!*' She plumped down, relieved. 'Haven't given it another thought.'

Barry couldn't be sure. But the relief in her voice sounded genuine.

'I'm going out,' he said.

'Going out are you? I bin telling Mrs Roebuck – do you all the good in the world being out all day. Only it's a bit late, the time you come in.' Her hesitation was almost apologetic, as though she realized he had grown older. 'I might stay out a bit myself, the odd night when no one's due for fitting. You won't mind, now you've got the playground? Me work's never done, but a change does me good.'

'You do that,' Barry shouted halfway through the door.

Next morning his mother shook him roughly awake.

'There's a letter come. From the headmaster. Jefferson School, it says.'

She handed him the letter and sat down breathing chestily.

Whatever the formalities – and Hal had told him to expect some – Miss Camperdown seemed to have got round them.

The letter simply said that the headmaster understood that she wished her son to attend the Jefferson School, and that, if this was so, half-term would be a convenient time for him to start. Since the half-term break was to begin in less than a week's time, the headmaster suggested an interview on Friday at five-thirty.

'That's tomorrow!' she exclaimed. 'And what does it mean, "Wish my son to attend"? Never heard of the place. How did they find out? Here've you bin hid away all these weeks, throwing fits whenever I tried to get you out, wouldn't see a doctor ...'

'I told you, Mum. There was some kids on the site.'

'Oh there's more to it than that!' she whirled around, standing in her doorway. 'Watching, they bin. Spying. No privacy these days. I *told* you –'

'Who then?'

'The police, the Welfare. Maybe, yes, blabbing the way you did, word got round . . . whatever made you?'

Barry kept silent.

Mrs Padgitt turned the letter over and over.

'We'll have to go I s'pose. Never any use fighting Them. Go and get it over.'

Saturday morning Barry was on the site before Hal and the rest got there. He wanted to tell Hal about his visit to the school; but after what Benjie had said he wondered if she'd be allowed to come?

The morning was cool, the sky overcast; a stillness hung over the leaves and grasses that were yet unspoiled, over the swing-rope and the half-erected hut, over the bushes that had been torn up last evening during his absence. Barry walked among them, searching for the place, now bare, where he and Hal had lain concealed. About a third of Hal's former territory had been left untouched, where the ground sloped and undulated too markedly for levelling to be feasible. The uprooted bushes lay like corpses after a battle. As he turned them over people began to arrive through the now accepted entrance at the side of the Institute. Hal was among them. Immediately an argument broke out as to what to do with the bushes.

'Pile them up in the middle and have a huge bonfire,' was Hal's suggestion. But Crimp Watson said his dad was coming tonight and how could he level the site for the five-a-sides unless it was cleared? At length the helper called Fred came from the hut and agreed with Crimp: the bushes would have to be carted away and could be piled up on the open grassy space.

As Hal, who had greeted him with the briefest nod, bent to grapple with a club-rooted privet, Barry said excitedly, 'I got in!'

She straightened: 'Come again?'

'School – I'm starting Monday week! In Miss Camperdown's class.'

'That's O.K., then.' She bent to pick up the bush and Barry couldn't tell if she was pleased or not. He worked alongside her, piling the bushes on the cart and pulling them away when it was loaded.

Later she asked, 'You saw the Head?' When Barry nodded she said, 'It was all right, then?'

Hal would have liked to ask him if he had found it very difficult, getting to the school, seeing the Head and that. But in the presence of others she didn't want to say too much. Didn't want to be 'paired off' with Barry. Getting him out of the house, getting him to meet Miss Camperdown had been enough. The finish, as far as she was concerned. He was no longer, as she had said to Miss Camperdown, 'on her mind'. Yet, watching him trying awkwardly to shift a scrubby, prickly furze bush, remembering their last encounter, deep among these very bushes, Hal began to foresee that this was only the beginning: she was stuck with Barry.

Later, when they were alone, she asked, 'The school – was it awful, getting there?'

Barry laughed: 'Mum took a taxi – she was more scared than me!' Of course he'd been scared – dead scared. But he wasn't going to let on.

'He was all right then, the Head?'

'Yeah, didn't say much.'

Relieved, Hal hurried off, leaving him to lie and watch the others.

The idea that he really *would* be starting at Jefferson was still unreal to Barry. Ten days before he needed to think about it.

Crimp Watson, still wearing his bush hat, his broad, bare back with its strong shoulder muscles bronzed by the sun, was bossing the site-clearers as once he had done his gang. Barry noticed that Hal ignored him, though Mary Malone stuck close by his side.

Young Benjie came out of his way to speak to Barry. 'His dad's coming tonight, five-thirty sharp, to level the pitches. Last night he brought a trench-digger so the men could lay pipes. Have you seen it – the trench? Over by the hut.'

Tim, now a whole-time play-leader, strolled over to have a word with Crimp. Barry was too far off to hear what they were saying, but he was struck by Crimp's defiant stance, chin up, chest out, legs apart, as though confronting Tim. Hal moved to Tim's side. Then the group broke up and Tim and Hal walked away.

Barry, feeling left out, got to his feet and turned his back on the lot of them. Even Anda and Bell no longer wanted to be with him – they were building a house against the air-vent wall with other younger children.

He passed the clump of trees where the rope swung out and back with a girl on the end, her legs pointed arrow-like, her feathered hair streaming behind her. Three boys were balancing along a telegraph pole, fixed about three feet up, parallel to the ground. Under Fred's supervision boys and girls were helping to nail roofing felt on the recreation hut, and council workmen were laying drains in the trench made by Crimp's father's machine. Everywhere there was activity, nothing, it seemed, for Barry to do.

He drifted along to the Institute gardens in search of Betty Pratt. Here, too, there was plenty going on, very little finished except a sand-pit where he saw Anda and Bell with kids of their own age. There was Kevin Pratt with a couple of older boys, patching up the door of an old shed. It looked as if the disused glasshouse had had broken panes replaced, though how long they'd stay unbroken, Barry thought, was anybody's guess. All over the site things were started by one lot of kids, broken up by another lot – this seemed to be accepted by everyone, along with the fights to get the stuff back, wood, bits of old cars, every imaginable kind of junk.

Maybe the garden, here, walled-in, was different, not thought of as part of the site? But Barry wasn't hopeful, and said as much when he found Betty working on what was to be a vegetable plot, skimming turves with a spade and turning them into a trench.

'I doubt it,' she replied, leaning on her spade. 'I mean, it's fun smashing things, isn't it? Chucking stones at glass especially.' She grinned. 'Admit it, you wouldn't mind having a go yourself!'

'I wouldn't, though – not the glasshouse. There's birds in it, aren't there?' Barry looked curiously at Betty. 'What's it in aid of, all this work, just to have it smashed? I don't mean things out there,' he jerked his head towards the site, 'bits and pieces – can be pulled down and started again. Even Hal's caff . . . You've heard about that? Her latest idea. She means to start a real caff – cook things. Charge money for it.'

Betty nodded, and Barry continued, 'But this work you're

doing here, it's real. Them lettuce seedlings over there – you'll be able to eat them. So why?'

Betty laughed. 'Search me,' she said. 'You make something because you feel like it – because it's fun. If it's spoilt you do it again, if you care enough. If not ...' She shrugged her shoulders and went to work once more. The work looked too heavy for her.

'I could get that up easier with a mattock,' he said, happy to display his growing strength.

'It'd be a help. The ground's too dry, and it's clay soil.'

She explained the process, and for a while they worked steadily, turning over trench after trench till the plot was finished. Then Barry fetched two bottles of fizzy orange from the recreation hut and they sat on the wall near the sandpit.

'What d'you think about Hal's caff?' he began, reintroducing the subject as a way of talking about her, 'd'you think it'll come off? She wants to put it where Crimp's hideout used to be. *That*'ll make him mad!'

'She's keen enough at the moment. And if the Georgiou boys stick to it and enough people help, it might. Hal's good at getting people to do things. She's always having new ideas. But she gets fed up and wants to go on to something else. Me, I hate cooking.'

Betty needed little prompting to discuss Hal. From their first day at Jefferson, she told him, she'd attached herself to Hal.

'The size of the place and the crowd of kids scared me stiff. I was always getting lost. I don't think I'd've stuck it without Hal – I really don't. Even now I might not. Did you know I've got a scholarship at the Royal College of Music? As well as being at Jefferson. It means extra hard work.'

As she spoke she drew off her gardening gloves and sat

absent-mindedly cracking her finger-joints, pulling them out and working them to make them supple.

Anda came up, covered with sand. 'Come and see the rabbits,' she said, leaning against Barry's knee.

'See rabbits,' echoed Bell, her damp nappy trailing behind her.

Betty tucked it in and brushed off the worst of the sand. The rabbits were in a shed, where the helper who ran the gardens was showing children how to feed them and clean out their hutches.

'We must make them a decent run,' she said, regarding Barry as a likely handyman. Her grey hair was cut short and she wore breeches and stockings, regardless of the heat. 'People are generous – or fed up with their pets. They bring them to us before we've made adequate provision for them. The budgies, now – they're in the glasshouse. If it hadn't been for your sixth-formers, Betty, working in the evenings, we'd never have got it mended in time.'

Anda pulled at Barry's hand and led him into the glasshouse. Here it was cool and the top lights had been painted green to keep out the sun's rays. The budgies were in a large cage to one side, and there were fresh branches stuck in beds of damp earth.

'Sometimes – only we have to be *very* careful – we shut the door and let them fly about,' Anda told Barry.

But Barry wasn't listening. His attention was fixed on a sudden apparition, a man's face, pressed close to one of the panes. A long, creased face with round, blue bloodshot eyes and yellow teeth that stuck out. Unhurriedly, the man turned away and made notes on the back of a cigarette packet.

'Who was that?' Betty looked startled.

'Search me. A right horror, I'd say. Those eyes – the way he looked at us!'

'It was worse than that. He wasn't looking at us. I mean, he wasn't *seeing* us.' Betty shivered. 'He looked a bit mad. A man like that about the place – it could spoil the site. The funny thing is, I think I've seen him before, or someone like him.'

'You're imagining things! He didn't see us 'cause he was working something out. It wasn't us he was interested in.'

All the same, Barry thought as he walked home across the site, Betty was right. That face – it'd give anyone the creeps. And seen like that, so unexpected. What was he after? Rabbit pie? Better keep an eye on the site, he thought, more than usual, at night when it was deserted.

Eleven

WHEN Barry came out after dinner he looked around for Hal and found her at last, with Betty, the Georgiou boys and others from her school, inside the semi-circular ruin on the hill that had been Crimp's. Tim was there too.

'We'd need something to cook on,' one of the Georgiou boys was saying. These two brothers were nuts about cooking.

Kevin hopped about on one foot in his excitement. 'We're going to have a caff – a real one! Charge people for food!'

'It'll be good,' Hal said, 'doing something real – not just playing around.'

Tim was examining the brick structure with the big window in it doubtfully. 'We'll have to make sure it's safe. Someone – go and get Fred over.'

'Benches round the walls . . .'

'A roof – it'll need roofing over . . .'

Just then Crimp, who had been working on the area set aside for the five-a-side pitches, shouldered his way through the group. He and others with him carried mattocks or picks on their shoulders.

Mary Malone had come up too, and stood near Crimp with folded arms and bent head, so that her hair fell over her face. She wore a short, faded sleeveless dress and her arms were milk-white, freckled by the sun. Barry, whose feelings were all for Hal, would yet have liked to take a gentle hold of Mary's arms simply because they were beautiful and gave him an idea of what the rest of her body was like. She was in two minds, he could see, from her quick uncertain look between Hal and Crimp.

'What's going on?' Crimp confronted Tim, standing squarely with his legs apart, his hands on his upturned mattock.

Everyone spoke at once: 'A caff – we're going to make a real caff!'

'This is my place,' Crimp said, still looking at Tim.

'Not now it isn't,' Hal interposed.

'It's my place.'

Hal moved closer to Tim. If Crimp was going to hit Tim he'd have to hit her first.

'That's up to you all,' Tim said, 'no use going for me.'

'You're supposed to be running the place.'

'No one's running the place. You're running it yourselves. I – and Fred and the other helpers – we're here to see you get what you want.'

'What I want,' Crimp rejoined belligerently, 'is for people to stick to what they're doing and not scarper off. My dad won't half carry on if he turns up and finds the five-a-sides not cleared.'

Fred, who had come up, took a tougher line. 'Where d'you get them picks? They're Council property. You know the rule – what was decided by us all. No tools without asking first. You must've broke open the toolshed.'

'Yeah – we broke it open while you was having lunch. No problem.'

'Drop all this about tools!' Tim, exasperated by Fred's bossy tactics, addressed the others. 'What about it? The guys that want to use the pitches – fair enough they should clear them?'

Reluctantly Benjie, Kevin and a few other boys detached themselves and followed Crimp downhill. Mary waited near Hal.

'Crimp's a queer bloke,' Barry remarked, 'he was one of the first to be in on the playground idea. Yet now it's going he doesn't much like it.'

'A trouble-maker,' was Fred's judgement. 'Make real trouble soon – he should be got off the site.'

But Tim shook his head. 'The site's for everyone. And he's strong – been no end of help clearing the place.'

Andreas Georgiou objected, 'But he's up against everyone, except his own gang.'

Mary spoke for the first time almost imploringly. 'You never ought to've taken his hide-out.'

Hal snorted. 'Hide-out! That's kid's stuff. We're making a proper caff, we're going to cook and charge money. Why don't you come and help, Mary?'

Mary shook her head. 'He'll never let you take his hide-out,' she repeated, with a heavy, sulky look. 'You don't understand Crimp. He's not a kid. He's older than any of you. He's all right only he won't stand for being messed around.'

There was an unaccustomed sadness in her voice; and puzzled defiance. Barry sensed a vague fear behind her words. He, too, felt a sense of foreboding. Crimp had left tension in the air.

Hal watched her go. 'I don't mind her being with Crimp's gang. But it seems to mean she can't be friends with us any more. Another thing – what I can't get is why he hates Tim so.'

Her mind was only partly on what she was saying. She was studying Tim, the way his reddish hair curled behind his ears and round the back of his neck. How would it feel, she wondered, to be kissed by a man with a beard? Tickly. She continued, 'Why does he always pick on you?'

'Does he?' Tim shrugged. 'In any group there are always guys who want to boss the rest, or who automatically oppose whoever they think is boss. Not that I feel like one!'

He turned to Fred. 'You've worked with a builder. Is this place safe?'

Fred, with a fair, stubbly beard, frayed jeans and bare feet like Tim, ran an expert hand and eye over the brickwork, his every movement eagerly followed by the Georgiou boys.

Fred thought it might be made safe enough, if strengthened, to bear a roof of sorts to keep the rain out. It would be open on one side. 'And the floor? That'll want screeding.'

'Barry knows how. He's been working on the recreation hut with the builders.'

'And you'll need more bricks. They're hard to come by.'

'We'll get bricks.' Barry spoke with such conviction that Hal felt confident too. Barry had no idea how they'd get bricks. Sand and cement they could get from the Council workmen still on the site. But bricks . . . 'It'll take time,' he said.

'There are so many things,' Betty Pratt said doubtfully, 'all happening at once. I ought to be helping with the gardens.'

'Gardens!' Hal's scorn was implied.

'I don't know,' Barry felt for Betty, 'they've got some budgies already. And rabbits. Nice for the kids.' He'd have quite liked to go along with Betty, if Hal hadn't been so keen on her new idea. 'They're growing useful stuff,' he said.

'Where's the money coming for that?' Hal asked jealously. Was she losing her hold over Betty as well as Mary?

She transferred her dissatisfaction to Tim. 'You're a bit soft, if you don't mind my saying so. Fred was better. Crimp – there are some people it's no use explaining to.'

Barry agreed. 'There are some blokes who – well, it's hard to say why, but it makes them all the madder if you try and make them see things your way, they feel sort of – got at. And they'll get back at you, given half a chance.'

'He's a proper worker,' Fred pointed out, 'I'll give him that. So long as there's things to be broken up, torn up, flattened. Building things, *making* things, that's different!'

'It's what I say,' Hal went on, 'you don't want to be soft. Take our Miss Camperdown . . .'

Tim looked at her so strangely that she stopped. '*Your* Miss Camperdown?' He gave Hal all his attention. 'You're going to say that she's not soft?'

'No. That's just it. Anyone who wastes her time – *our* time – she won't stand for it.'

'So I can imagine!' Tim sounded bitter. Hal felt affronted: no one was going to pass remarks on Campers – not someone who didn't know her.

Before she could answer Benjie ran up and broke in: 'Hey mister!'

'Tim,' Hal corrected him, 'we're not in school now.'

Ignoring her Benjie cried, 'Crimp's pinched a ladder!'

Looking back the way Benjie had come, Tim frowned. 'O.K. Maybe he needs one.'

'He's up on the brick thing – the railway thing!'

But Tim had already started to run.

A crowd had gathered round the old brick air-vent. On its rim, Crimp balanced, pretending to sway, recovering himself. Uneasy laughter rose and died away. When Tim reached the ladder's foot one of Crimp's gang was already halfway up and another had his foot on the bottom rung. Tim shoved him aside and began to mount. 'Come down!'

The boy on the ladder looked round, half-afraid, not unwilling to be stopped. Tim grabbed his ankle.

The boy kicked out, but he came down. Then Tim went up, bare toes curling on the rungs. Crimp danced away from him. As he set foot on the brick rim Tim went after him, Hal saw with horror, unsteadily. Crimp saw too, and smiled. He stood on the opposite side of the air-vent, his thumbs in the waistband of his jeans, as though uncertain what to do next. Slowly Tim came after him. He looked, Hal could see, as green as Barry the first time she'd seen him.

'Don't look,' Barry said behind her.

But Hal kept her eyes on Tim, willing him to be all right. If she looked away for a second, she felt, he'd go over. With her whole body she willed him not to fall.

Fred now stood at the foot of the ladder.

'Quiet!' he looked around him, but there was no need: laughter had changed to a murmur, murmur to silence.

'Get him down – oh! go up quick,' Hal whispered, 'can't you see?'

'Yes. But it might make things worse.'

In the silence a low rumble was heard, quickly growing to a roar. A train was coming. It seemed as though the whole structure shook. Tim swayed. Instantly Crimp was by his side, pointing outwards. He had Tim by the wrist, steadying him, turning him away from the black pit, making him sit down, sitting beside him. When the train had passed Fred went up and together they worked Tim round, still sitting, till the ladder was reached.

When he was safely on the ground Hal heard him say, 'Never had a head for heights.' He put his face in his hands, then looked up and saw Crimp.

'You won't do that again,' he said faintly.

'No,' said Crimp.

'He won't have a chance!' Fred was ready to march him off the site forthwith, and Crimp would have gone.

'No!' Tim's voice was stronger. He got to his feet. 'We'll give it another try?' He looked at Crimp, who nodded.

'We'll have to get British Rail to put something solid up there – wire it in – in case anyone else tries it. Or the Council will have to.' They were starting to walk back to the hut. Hal and Barry and one or two others followed them.

'You saved his life!' Hal heard Mary say, and turned back, full of anger. Crimp stood apart from the rest, frowning at the ground, screwing his heel into the turf. 'You moron!' he said savagely, 'I very nearly killed him.'

'What was there in the hole?' Kevin asked.

'Blackness. There was some netting near the top but it was rusty. All right to stop birds...'

'You look real bad,' Barry said to Hal. 'Come and have a cup of tea?'

Hal let herself be taken to the recreation hut. She was weak and ached all over.

'You sit down outside. I'll get you a sandwich as well.'

She shook her head. 'Tea would be nice.'

They sat with their backs against the hut and drank the sweet tea.

After waiting for a bit he said, 'I bin thinking. There must be hundreds of bricks around with all them houses coming down. Why not take a barrow or a cart or something and look for some?'

Hal was impressed. 'You could do that?' She looked at his long skinny legs stretched out on the grass and remembered how recently he had found walking difficult.

'Sure.' He wasn't in the least sure, but determined to keep Hal's interest. 'It only means looking around. Make a hand-cart first, we might have to.'

Hal explained she meant was he well enough? Of course he was, Barry told her: he was getting stronger every day, just as Tim had said he would.

'Swimming's the best for your muscles,' Barry went on, 'I go with Tim quite often. Gives me exercises, too.'

'*Tim* does?' Hal felt a stab of jealousy. 'Takes you swimming?'

'Why don't you come too? We could go early before school.'

'Yeah, I will.' Then she remembered Anda and Bell. And sat silent, head down, hands hanging between her knees.

Barry had never seen Hal like this. He wanted to put his arm round her, but they weren't alone and he guessed she wouldn't like it. Gently he got her to talk – about Anda and Bell, and their mum working early mornings, the distance from the Centre to the school and how they were always on her hands, the kids, Benjie being a lazy beast and a boy at that so their mum let him off anything, any time.

She spoke with such passion and despair that Barry stared at her.

'You've never minded like this before – I mean you've not felt like this all the time?'

She lifted her head. 'Maybe not, but –'

'And the site – coming here makes it easier, surely?'

'Yeah. Course it does. But when I want to do something special . . .'

'Don't you go swimming with the school?'

'That's not the same.'

She imagined swimming with Tim. He would teach her to dive, as she had seen fathers do with their children. She would sit on his shoulders and he would tip her over, carefully at first . . .

'Are you O.K.? Have you got a pain?' Barry's anxiety was mixed with a pleasing sense of being needed.

Hal sat staring ahead: 'Yeah. Sort of.'

She felt it in her chest and tummy, where it stopped her breathing. She felt it in all her being. She watched Tim cross the grass; and something inside her melted. She would never be able to tell anyone what she felt about Tim. No one would ever know.

She gave a great sigh and turned over on her front, where she lay stretched out.

'Maybe something you ate? That sandwich?'

'Nah!' She lifted her head, 'I'm O.K.'

'You can go swimming before school,' Barry was saying. 'I promise.' Nothing, at that moment when she seemed to need him, seemed impossible. 'I'll come, say, one morning, and take Bell to the Centre. Why not?'

' 'Cause you don't live anywhere near!' She laughed and sat up.

'We'll get them bricks,' he said urgently. 'We'll get a cart made, a handcart, and go looking.'

Twelve

BEFORE the half-term holiday had ended Barry had become more and more at ease with the others, even with boys of his own age, specially after some of them in Hal's class heard he was coming to Jefferson. For the first time in his life he found himself one of a friendly group. At his previous schools he had not made many friends; for one thing he was always changing schools.

And there was something about him that attracted bullies. It had begun long ago, when someone had recognized him on a hoarding, a little mannikin wearing a pale blue coat with a velvet collar; before he left that school he had learned to hate and fear everyone in it, an experience that made him wary and unresponsive wherever else he went. Mostly, teachers learnt to leave him alone, as did the children, except for the tormentors there are in every school.

But on the site things were different. As Hal said, 'You can do your own thing,' and everyone did, so that Barry began to lose his self-consciousness and live alongside others without feeling singled out, nor, on the other hand, excluded.

He even began to make friends of his own apart from Hal, like the two Greek boys, Dimitri and Andreas Georgiou. Their father kept a butcher's shop, and once, when they'd been out with the handcart scrounging bricks from a derelict area near by, the boys took Barry in to rest and have a cool drink. The shop itself was refreshingly cool, with white walls and coloured streamers in the doorway to keep out flies.

Mrs Georgiou made Barry sit down while her husband and his two elder sons who helped him in the shop scraped the wooden chopping blocks clean and washed down the walls. There were holy pictures hanging behind the steel racks from which joints of meat were hooked down and put in a cold store.

'See what we've got out in the yard!' Dimitri said triumphantly. It was an old stove, rusty, but still good for cooking on, and they wanted to load it up on the handcart right away, emptying out the bricks for a further load. But Mrs Georgiou said no: they should take their friend home in the cart.

'He has been ill. He has walked enough for one day.'

'*Ill?*' cried Dimitri, 'you don't know, mama! You don't *know* how he kept on at us when Andreas and I wanted to stop because of the heat. We had looked and looked, but there were no bricks. "Bricks," we said, "where are these bricks?" And he said, "I don't know. But we shall find some." And he kept pulling the cart when we wouldn't, up and down those streets that are all boarded up. So how could we leave him, the madman?'

'And in the end we found some,' put in his brother. 'A house had fallen down at one end, there were trees growing through the roof. All on its own in a garden. There are plenty more if we can get back quick enough.'

The two boys looked at their mother, and back at Barry with affectionate pride.

Mrs Georgiou smiled, shaking her head. 'Was it so important, these bricks? Worth getting ill again?'

Barry explained, 'It was a promise. But I could never have got them without Dimitri and Andreas. And I don't feel ill, just a bit tired.' He turned to the boys. 'Let's empty out the bricks and take the stove. And come back for another load – or you can. Just think what Hal will say when she sees the stove!'

'Now it's like a real caff!' Hal said two days later, when the stove had been rubbed down and cemented into the centre of the ruined brick bay. Smoke poured from its tin chimney, sheltered by walls that were as yet half-built. Barry had screeded the floor, extending it to make a terrace.

'We'll make benches and tables!' cried Dimitri, pretending to be a waiter with a tray held high on his finger-tips.

'Funny thing,' Barry remarked as they sipped their smokey tea, 'I made sure Crimp would come over and wreck every bit we did. Every evening I've watched out. He was so mad when we took over his place.'

'He's lost interest, building his tower is all he thinks about.'

Through the unglazed window in the curved wall they could look across to the furthest corner of the site. There, on high ground, Crimp and his gang had begun to build a tower with odd lengths of wood, snitched, it was said, from his father's yard. When finished it would overlook the canal like a watchtower. From time to time they nicked wood from the 'houses' built by the younger kids, provoking an enraged howl and an ineffectual skirmish. But as Barry remarked, the kids were always pinching from each other, their houses always in process of rebuilding and falling down on their own.

'Mary Malone's doing all right!' commented Dimitri.

There were no girls in Crimp's gang except Mary, who wasn't much good at humping wood; she had taken to wearing a long trailing dress of crushed pink velvet and a headband low on her forehead. But she was not required to do much, only to admire Crimp, which she could quite well do lying gracefully on a patch of grass as yet untrampled, while at intervals the boys provided food and drink cooked on their own fire, charred sausages, blackened potatoes, tea with water boiled in an old tin can.

Crimp fascinated Barry. He couldn't make him out. He wasn't a slob, he wasn't actually a bully, though he had the air of being one, poised on the edge of violence. He wasn't a man, though, for all he was short, he had the musculature of a man.

'It's not that he's stupid,' Barry said aloud, 'yet he can't take in anything Tim says, seems not to understand.'

'He's still got it in for Tim,' said Dimitri.

'And why?' cried Hal.

'Maybe because he's stronger than Tim,' one of the boys suggested. 'Crimp could knock him down easy. That's why he likes Fred better – takes notice of what he says.'

'He goes to a special school,' Hal said. 'Mary told me. A posh private place where they only have four or five people to a teacher. He hates his dad, Mary said.'

'Not surprising,' Barry commented. 'Ever seen him close to?' For it had come to him that the fishy-eyed snooper peering into the greenhouse was none other than Crimp's dad. He'd seen him from afar, from his window, working the bulldozer when the five-a-sides were cleared. But it was only now that he identified him. 'There he is now, coming this way.'

Mr Watson was heavily built, made squarer by the short, fur-collared coat he wore, in spite of the heat. He was never seen without a little round hat with a narrow brim. He looked towards them, up the steep slope. He must have been able to see them staring at him through the window. But he wasn't interested, Barry pointed out, not enough to come up the track and round the back and see what they were doing.

'I don't believe he's even seen us,' said Hal. 'Doesn't he want to come round and see the caff? Maybe he doesn't know there's a way round, easy to walk up.'

Barry shook his head. 'He's not looking at us. It's the place – I dunno, but look at his eyes. They're screwed up, like he was measuring something.'

'Calculating,' agreed one of the Georgiou boys.

'A right skate,' said his brother, 'that big mouth full of teeth – makes him look as though he was smiling all the time.'

'Which he's not,' said Hal. 'No wonder Crimp hates him. They're on their own. No mum, Mary says.'

They all felt vaguely uneasy.

'He's been round late,' Barry said. 'Other blokes with him. Walking around the place – the part that's bin left wild.'

'He can't do anything,' commented Dimitri. 'We bin promised the site, by the Council and all.'

'There's nothing it could be used for.'

Barry got up. 'Better be making tracks,' he said. 'Mum'll be home and she gets mad if I'm late for supper these days. Then she can get out afterwards. Always going out these days she is.'

'Maybe she's got a date,' laughed one of the boys.

'You can say that again! A feller with plenty of cash, too. She doesn't tell me and I don't ask.'

Barry's new detachment was genuine. He was relieved that his mum seemed to have something going for her. It took her mind off him, while it lasted. Somehow Mrs Padgitt's boy-friends never did last, but the feller who was taking her out now made her feel good, you could see. Bought her new clothes, took her up west, called for her in a slinky car – he'd spotted it waiting at the street corner. True enough, sometimes she gave him a guilty, almost sad look which puzzled him. But he was too full of his own affairs to wonder overmuch about hers.

'Anyhow, I want to keep her sweet – I told you about that new school she's so mad about?'

They nodded, and set to work as Barry left them.

On his way back Barry stopped to watch a boy swinging, out and back, on the rope that hung from the tall sycamore. Nearby three boys, all Crimp's pals, were doing a balancing act along an old telegraph pole. Suddenly the boy slipped down the rope, and was hanging from the wooden wedge by his legs. Back and forth he swung, then, leaving the rope and turning a somersault in the air, landed like a parachute jumper, a yard or two from Barry.

Thinking he must be hurt, Barry ran to his side. But already he was on his feet, grinning. Barry grinned back, 'That was terrific!'

The other three had joined them.

'His dad's in a circus,' cried one, and they all laughed raucously. 'Come on – 'ave a go!'

'Not me!' Barry was still smiling. But a note in their laughter wiped the smile off his face. 'We'll teach yer,' one grabbed his arm, 'cissy-boy!' The baying of their derision made his mind blank with terror.

'Come on, softie!'

The four of them went for him. Barry wrenched free, hit out and poked one in the belly. What followed happened so quickly that there was no time for fear. He went limp – an old trick he had learnt at his last school, only now he wasn't strong enough to follow it up, could only lie there with them on top of him.

Suddenly they stopped punching, separated, stood around uncertainly. Crimp stood above him.

'Can't you see the creep's sick? What's the point?'

While he waited Barry got to his feet, and managed to walk away.

'Are ye all right?' Mary murmured behind him.

' 'Course,' he answered gruffly.

Barry didn't like Crimp any better for what he had done; wouldn't forget the contempt in his voice as he had stood above him. Nor was he grateful for the part Mary had played in Crimp's intervention, a little drama enacted, he felt sure, for her benefit.

But as he walked unsteadily on he felt a curious sense of relief. The worst had happened: he had not run away; and the reality was nothing like so bad as his nightmare imaginings.

Feet thudded behind him. It was the Georgiou boys.

'We never saw,' they cried, 'what happened? Someone told us you were in a fight! Who was it? Crimp's gang?' They looked round defiantly. But Barry's assailants had trailed off, unwillingly, behind Crimp. 'It's O.K.,' Barry got out, through swollen lips, 'didn't last long.' They walked him back to his garden wall, protectively. He climbed the wall, unaided, and managed a smile. They might think he'd beaten the gang single-handed. It was only later that he reflected that Mary would probably give Hal the true version.

That evening, Barry, stiff and sore, didn't go down again after supper. Mrs Padgitt, half-alarmed, half-impressed by Barry's account of his single-handed fight, had offered to stay in. But on Barry's assurance that he really liked being on his own, she went off, wearing a new satin evening coat with monkey fur round the hem.

Barry sat by the window, looking down on the site. The asphalted football pitches were crowded, the crazy lean-to's round the 'volcano' almost deserted as the younger children drifted off home. To the right, smoke rose lazily from Hal's caff into the windless evening air. Beyond that was the Institute and its gardens, hidden from his view, but no doubt Betty would be there and the elderly helper in breeches and woollen stockings.

Occasionally Barry had deserted Hal's caff and gone off to the gardens. He wasn't crazy about the prospect of cooking. And he suspected that Hal wasn't either. What attracted her was the idea of doing something 'real'. The Georgiou boys could be relied on to do the hard work once they opened up. Barry went off to see Betty Pratt; he'd first taken to her because of her friendship with Hal, then for her own sake. She was passive where Hal was dominant, an escape from Hal when she was too demanding. Barry liked the way Betty listened to him, intently, through large round glasses. And he learnt from her – about animals and plants, and names to remember, like Rose Bay Willow Herb: 'It's like a girl's name,' he said. There was so much to see and remember and find out about, in ways he'd never thought of before.

At least two-thirds of the site was still left wild; and it was this part, Barry observed, that seemed to interest Crimp's father most. For there he was at this moment with two men, on a hillock crowned with ash saplings where Barry himself had often lain. He was sizing up the prospect before him in a way Barry had come to resent. For he couldn't believe that Mr Watson was around because he liked to see kids enjoying themselves – it just wasn't possible: you had only to look at him. And Crimp – was he in his watchtower? His dad, as far as Barry had seen, never took notice, seemed almost to avoid Crimp's small corner, never went up that way. But then Mary had told Hal Crimp hated his dad. More: her idea was that they hated each other, never spoke unless his dad had something nasty to say. But you couldn't believe half Mary said, any more than you could Crimp.

The men had left the hillock, only to reappear up on one of the winding, bush-choked trails that led nowhere. They were making, these city-dressed intruders, in a roundabout way towards the brick air-vent. They looked up as if guessing its height. One man gave a contemptuous kick at one of the wooden 'houses' at its base. The lean-to fell down, and they walked off, leaving exposed a box-table, a small pile of bricks, a broken jam-jar with flowers fallen out of it, a ruin. What could they possibly find of interest on Barry's site? (For he still thought of it as his, specially when he saw it from his window, as of old. It couldn't be built on, they'd been promised it by the Council – he told himself over and over. Yet still he felt a sense of threat, of danger, brooding over the site like the brazen clouds that seemed to sag lower and lower as night drew on and the place emptied and was still.

Tomorrow was the last day of the half-term holiday; soon the site would be empty all day. And he wouldn't be there to watch over it.

This reflection gave way to a colder, more realistic, quite sickening realization – one that he'd successfully kept out of mind this past week. Tomorrow he was going to Hal's school.

Thirteen

On Barry's first morning at Jefferson Hal met him by arrangement near the school. By an extraordinary effort of organization she had got Bell to the Centre and herself to the meeting-place before Barry arrived. Would he ditch her at the last moment? When she saw him rounding the corner by the butcher's, swinging his way in a purposeful manner through travellers queueing for buses and bunching to cross the road to the Underground, she could almost have hugged him from relief.

'Hullo!' he nodded, hardly pausing in his course, so that she had to stride out to keep up with him. Glancing sideways she saw what Mary had seen – that Barry was potentially a 'good-looker' with his well-shaped head and his long fair hair blown in the breeze of a fine summer morning. Automatically he put up a hand to push it back, looking all the while straight ahead. If only his eyes and his mouth didn't narrow into slits! If they had been alone Hal would have touched his face with a finger as she had done that evening in the bushes; he would have been transformed. But they were not alone; and as they approached the school she said, 'Slow down a bit, can't you? Everyone'll be looking at us!'

Barry slackened his pace; they had joined a stream of boys and girls making for the school gates. But he kept his eyes on the building ahead with its jutting bastions and windows reflecting the level sunlight.

On the steps the Georgiou boys hailed him. 'Show you the locker room?' Andreas took him by the elbow and the three of them left Hal for sunless corridors snaked with pipes, funnelling a low, growing murmur that became a stunning roar as they entered the locker rooms. No one among the hundreds of boys gave Barry more than a passing glance. 'That's your number,' Dimitri explained, indicating a coat hook, 'everyone has a number, you're supposed to have it sewn on your things as well as your name, but no one does.' And he was shown a boot-hole where he would keep his football boots and P.T. shoes when he had them.

'Aren't there no lockers?' Barry asked, the first words he had spoken.

'No, things get nicked all the time.'

They seemed unconcerned; but for Barry the lack of this minimal privacy, combined with the noisy crowd, was a setback. He wanted to get out quickly, before inner panic took over.

By contrast Form IVb's room, when they got there, was quiet and seemed almost empty, though a dozen or more children were already assembled and active. The height of the room and the tall east-facing window filled with blue sky made Barry stand still, blinking; then he saw Miss Camperdown, who greeted him in a friendly way and said she supposed he would like to be a 'Lollard', the same as Hal and Betty and Andreas and Dimitri, and a good many others whom he recognized and who accepted him without surprise since they had met him in the playground and expected him. Soon the room was filled up with forty or more girls and boys.

It was as Hal had foretold; no one singled him out for special attention. They soon discovered that he could draw and paint, and Hal saw to it that he was given exotic birds to copy, in all their intricate detail and colour, lifesize, to go on the history comp screen.

However daunting the experience of finding yourself in a totally new situation, its very unfamiliarity can work powerfully against feelings of fear and withdrawal. You begin to anticipate; you want to go on to the next thing. The smells of fresh paper, of lead pencil and paints sharpened Barry's perceptions; and after he had concentrated for a while on his painting he began to take in his surroundings, to see Mary Malone kneeling on the floor with her hair falling round an outsize book, and Betty Pratt, with a gesture that had become familiar, standing back, with her head on one side, biting her little finger, considering how best to pin something up. Miss Camperdown, he noticed, was wearing a mini-skirt of some light material, and long boots – sweaty, they must be in summer. He would not want Hal's long legs encased in boots. Hal, catching his look, noticed that the slitty eyes and mouth had relaxed; he gave her a wide smile and she smiled back.

This sense of anticipation carried him through the whole day; it was like a new taste on his tongue. He even ate his lunch with relish. Told Springy he, Barry, knew what mangoes tasted like. And fairly confronted the maths teacher because her method of working out a problem was different from his.

'I got the answer right, didn't I?' he challenged her. Afterwards he told Hal and some others that they were taught very old-fashioned.

'Maybe, but – ' Hal's impulse was to cut him down to size. Then, marvelling at his spirit, she decided to leave his cheek alone. It was his first day.

Everyone who had known Barry on the site was surprised; they had begun to share Hal's attitude to him, a mixture of proprietory concern and curiosity – proprietory because they had seen him grow better, felt somehow they had a hand in his improvement, curious because he was like a plant in a pot found on a window-sill, watered fed and transplanted, a nameless plant. What would it grow into?

'It won't last,' Dimitri said wisely, talking like his father, who read a lot in between running the shop, and conversed with his sons like grown-ups.

'Why shouldn't it?' Hal spoke defensively. But she had a hunch Dimitri was right.

She and the brothers were standing on the school steps at the day's end.

Dimitri shrugged his shoulders. Then he pretended to blow up a paper bag and burst it. 'He'll go off pop.'

'Or just crumble.' Andreas let the air out of an imaginary balloon.

'Nurts!' Hal ran down the steps and caught up with Barry on his way to the gates with Mary and Betty.

At the traffic lights they parted; it was natural for Barry and Hal to go the same way, and Hal had lost her sense of embarrassment at being paired off with him since now he promised to do her credit.

'Like to come home with me?' she asked at the parting of their way.

'Yeah. P'raps not today.' Exhaustion was beginning to overtake him. 'Maybe at the weekend?'

Hal, on her way home, thought better of the impulse. She had never brought a boy home before and didn't much want to now. She had no idea how her parents would take this new move, specially her dad. What bugged her was the idea of Barry's going back alone to that flat high up, his mother as likely as not out. But why should he? They had the site going – a better place to meet.

Barry didn't, as Dimitri had foretold, 'go off pop.' His elation carried him home, lasted while he lay on his bed and watched his mother get their supper. From time to time she gave him a searching look as he lay with his hands behind his head, his eyes bright and staring, his mouth wide and slightly parted. 'How was it?' she would ask. Or, 'Was it very bad – your first day?' And he would answer absently, 'O.K.' or, 'It was all right.'

'You're miles away,' she said, as indeed he was, with the whole day – all its sights and sounds and smells – whirling in his head.

'D'you want to eat?' she asked.

With an effort Barry rolled off his bed and joined her at the small table. They were suffocatingly close together. Barry had the feeling that she wanted to take something from him, scoop out the past day with all its memories, and leave him empty. The sensation was unbearable, the more so because, as Barry could dimly perceive, an outsider would see only his mum, picking at her egg and chips, her face work-worn, eyes creased at the corners, anxious and uncertain, but in no sense predatory.

'I can't seem to get anywhere near you these days,' she said with her eyes lowered, 'you never tell me what you do.'

Barry pushed away his plate.

'You've left your chips . . .'

'I ate so much dinner,' he said, and detailed what he had eaten. 'You won't have to spend so much on our tea, nothing like.' Wanting to tell her something, he followed up this easier theme. 'And now you don't have to come home you can get a good dinner yourself in the works canteen. It's real good, the school dinners, you can have vegetarian if you like. Betty Pratt does.'

'You never spoke about her. Never talk about any of your friends, come to that. She your girlfriend?'

His mother leant forward and Barry jumped up, knocking his chair over. 'I've told you, Mum, we all go around together. You've seen us on the site – it's the same lot, more or less, at school.'

'Don't think I mind you having a girlfriend,' she spoke appealingly. 'Kids start young these days. It's only that I'd like to know. I've a right. I mean you wouldn't want one of them foreigners with their different ways ...'

'But I haven't got a girlfriend, honest, Mum.' He couldn't be sure Hal was his girlfriend, he couldn't begin to guess what her feelings for him were, except that they were changeable. Above all, whatever there was between them, his mum mustn't know. Putting it into words – her words – could spoil it for good and all.

He sat down on the bed and put his head in his hands. 'I'm flaked out.'

He began to pull his shirt over his head. She sat down beside him.

'You poor love,' she crooned, prepared for him to put his head on her shoulder. But he pulled away and sat pressed against the wall, hugging his knees, his blue eyes wide and cold. They stared at one another and without a word spoken it was understood that he was too old: she must never try to kiss and hold and comfort him again.

She turned away and began to tidy up. Her words were hostile, her voice husky with her endless fag-smoking. 'It's that awful school – of course you're tired out – ill again I shouldn't wonder – much too big, and a rough lot most of them – it'll make you ill, you'll never stand it!'

She was turned away from him, her hands resting on the prospectus of the boarding school. 'You mark my words – you'll be on your back tomorrow!'

So powerful was she that Barry was persuaded: he felt the illness returning. But he braced himself against the wall and cried: 'I'm not leaving – I'm staying at Jefferson. Get that!'

She came nearer; he saw tears on her cheeks.

'I only want what's best for you. It's all I've ever wanted.'

'I know that. I really do, Mum.'

She went away. Soon he heard the telly switched on. He got into bed in his underpants and slept at once.

As sometimes happens when you are overtired, he woke with a jerk. Tossed and turned but couldn't sleep again.

The telly was silent; but his mother's light was on, and he heard stealthy movements; she wasn't in bed yet, late though it was. Her last words came back to him, and he felt sorry. For she had meant what she said: 'I only want what's best for you.'

He heard a drawer slide open. He got out of bed and opened her door. She was kneeling in front of the open drawer. Socks, underpants, striped pyjamas – they were all there, carefully laid away. At the bottom of the layers the blazer was hidden. As he entered she held it up.

'The same as what they wear in the House of Lords,' she said, seeing him, 'except it's green, not red. Mrs Roebuck's husband's brother – its his firm makes the cloth, so she should know.'

Barry was speechless. As he saw her now, she was completely mad. These clothes meant everything to her: 'I only want what's best for you.'

She closed the drawer and put the key in her purse.

Trying reason, Barry said, 'But I go to Jefferson. That's my school.'

She leant back on her heels. 'Jefferson! How long d'you think that'll last? Nasty rough lot of boys there'll be there. You'll soon give up going, same as you did other schools, once they set on you.'

'But they don't.'

'Not that it's any surprise to me, your getting bullied. It's because you're different from them, the way I always meant you to be. Kept you nice, clean, and with good clothes. Well-spoken. Never mind what it cost me.'

She was off, talking, railing as she hadn't done for weeks. One day Barry would understand what it had meant, bringing a kid up on her own, paying for a baby-minder, taking overtime work home. Dodging the Welfare, once even, when she'd got deep in debt, the police – everyone had wanted to take him from her, but she'd held out.

Barry had ceased to listen to this old stuff, though it left a load of guilt somewhere in his mind.

She got to her feet: 'Not that I'm one to waste time moaning about the past. Those years weren't wasted. I knew something special would turn up – and here it is. Cranmere College!'

She was positively jubilant – as though Jefferson didn't exist.

Fourteen

BUT Mrs Padgitt, it seemed, was wrong about Barry and Jefferson School. Getting there was the hardest part – getting himself out of the house, after his mum had left for work. But once in the school, through the iron gates, the heavy doors, the sweaty, subterranean changing rooms – once in IVb classroom, Barry's stomach stopped churning, his breath came easier as his mind settled on whatever they were doing; it didn't seem to matter what. No one looked at him specially, except when he was late, and then only with a nod. No one went for him.

Barry was very often late; he nearly always missed Assembly, a gathering of the whole school in a vast hall. At first it worried him, when he sidled into the classroom after Assembly was over, Campers' eye on him, and her saying nothing. Like his mother, he sensed that she was biding her time; well, he could wait too. See how long he could get away with it. Barry had been 'getting away' with things all his life. You could always get ill, he had found. In the end, people – teachers got tired of trying.

At first there were days he never came at all. Days spent in the playground, sloping around, being given jobs to do by Tim, talking to the men still on the site. Pretending he'd had an ordinary school day when his mother came home at night, writing his own 'excuse letter' the next day.

The third time this happened, Miss Camperdown called him back after the others had gone out.

She scrumpled up the 'excuse letter'. 'No more of these,' she said shortly, 'no lies. Assembly – you can miss that. Some people are allowed to miss it – can't stand crowds, faint or get sick. If it goes on, your not being able to stand Assembly, we'll try and do something about it. Just now it's unimportant. But come to school you must!' She looked at him compellingly. 'Not just because of the others, though that could be bad. I mean, once people begin playing truant ... No. It's because of you. *For* you. Jefferson was your choice. If you can't get here no one's going to make you. Or help you. You must help yourself. This is something between you and me. If you can get here I'll keep you. Otherwise ...'

She did not need to finish. Barry thought of Cranmere College, a great bottomless hole waiting for him to fall into.

'I'll come,' he said, 'I'll go on coming.'

And he did.

That was the day the play for the school Open Day was first talked about. The three groups in IVb were all in corners, discussing what they would do. Every class had to do something. Most classes were given a plan, prepared and drilled by their form-teachers. But Campers and Springy – oh no! Lollards, Luddites and Levellers, each had to do their own thing.

'It's *your* Open Day, isn't it?' Campers had said, reminding them that, as usual, time was getting short. 'It's you your parents come to see – what *you* can do, not us.' She glanced towards Springy, who had come to take over for the next period.

So it was that the Lollards huddled together in their corner, while Hal and the Georgiou brothers and Betty explained to newer arrivals that they had all got to think – and think fast.

Every now and then a boy or a girl would run over to Springy, who had taken up his favourite position on the teacher's dais and was squatting there on the edge with his hands hanging between his knees as though ready to spring. He lent a ready ear to all suggestions, nodding or shaking his head, waving an arm towards the bookcase, shrugging his shoulders.

'He's beginning to look bored,' whispered Mary Malone. 'No one's come up with anything – nothing really good.'

'Do *think*,' moaned Betty. 'We've got the screen, and all the flowers, and the birds Barry painted . . .'

'What else?' asked Barry. 'Isn't that enough?'

'We have to act something – sing something.'

'About what we've been doing,' put in Dimitri, 'the slave trade.'

Hal had a brainwave. 'Some of you,' she cried, forgetting to be quiet, 'people from Africa – must know songs – songs you sing at home. My dad – he says that's where we came from, the African coast.' She stopped to think. 'Maybe it seems silly, now, I mean, all so long ago.'

'Go on,' Barry said, 'doesn't sound silly.' He looked around. No one thought it sounded silly. *Any* idea . . .

'Well, Dad knows songs – he comes from Barbados. Doesn't sing them now. But I remember when I was a kid . . .'

This was as far as Hal could go. She'd had an idea. But it didn't seem to lead anywhere. Just *songs* – even if her Dad could remember the words, and she suspected he'd long forgotten them.

Her glance at Barry was an appeal for help.

'Songs,' he ruminated, 'dances?' He looked inquiringly at

an African girl. She clapped her hands in delight, was ready to get to her feet and show them all how she danced, how they danced at home in Nigeria.

'Go on,' Barry said, 'yeah, it's an idea.'

The girl jumped up and began to dance. A Kenyan boy beat a rhythm on the floor. Others joined in. More Lollards leapt to their feet, dancing, beating, clapping. It hardly lasted five minutes: remembering where they were they collapsed in a heap, laughing, laughing so they couldn't stop. Mary hugged the girl who had begun it, 'You were great!'

In the silence that followed, they became aware of the other two groups, every head turned their way. Then, as though they could not bear to be out of it, a low beating of hands began, chanting, a bedlam of songs. Then everyone was on their feet, Pakistanis, Cypriots – the lot. Mary Malone was dancing a jig, with her own mouth-music. Only the English stood about, envious, embarrassed. A door banged, loud enough to stop them. Miss Camperdown stood just inside, looking at Springy, who had been doing a soft-shoe shuffle round the desk on the daïs.

'That's about *it*,' she muttered, striding into the middle of the room, 'that's all we needed.' She looked back at Springy. He had taken off his burning-bright tie, and now began winding it back on again.

'If I hadn't been teaching next door . . .'

Everyone knew what Campers meant. Her kind of teaching – and Springy's – wasn't popular with most of the staff. If she, and the staff who agreed with her, couldn't persuade more of the others to use what Miss Blunt called, with acid sarcasm, her 'methods', the head would have to come down in the end on what Springy had called 'the side of reaction'. That would mean – Campers had said it herself – her leaving.

So IVb had tried with all their might to show that her kind of teaching, worked. More, they tried, when they remembered, to be polite and quiet when they were in what Barry once called 'the enemy camp'. Maths, and English language, for instance.

They really had tried, specially this second half of the term, for Campers had made it plain that she was under pressure to change her ways by the end of the school year. Or rather, Springy had made it plain, plainer and more often than was helpful to Campers. IVb were attached to Springy, not just because of his loyalty to Campers, but because they liked his teaching – her way. Only they could not keep quiet during his periods. They just *could not*.

Anyhow, here she was silent with rage in the middle of the floor. Springy stepped down and joined her.

'It wasn't his fault, miss,' Hal spoke up, as though Springy was one of themselves, 'it was my idea. Us singing songs.'

'*Songs!*' burst out Miss Camperdown. 'It was like Wembley on Cup Final Day. How could you? How could any of you?'

Barry said (and could never have explained what prompted him), 'It's a play. We want to do a play. About the slave trade.'

A play! All eyes were on Barry. A low murmur ran round the room. Then, suddenly, it became clear that a play was what they had all been wanting to do all along, without knowing it. The whole of IVb closed up round Campers and Springy, clamouring to do a play. In an instant Campers had quelled the riot: 'No reason why not,' she said, when she'd made them sit down just where they were on the floor. 'But you'll have to do an awful lot of thinking – not shouting. And an awful lot of work. Four weeks left till Open Day. How about it, Mr Springer? Worth trying?

She walked towards the door: 'It's all yours,' she looked back at him, 'drama's your department.'

Springy, it appeared, had been to drama school back home in the States. Several minutes passed while he paced the dusty floor, concentrating in thought as the class had never seen him before, pinching his chin, twisting a finger in his little soft side-whiskers, pulling off his tie as though it stopped him thinking.

Then he began to change, as though he were different people. Sometimes he walked one way, slow, painfully, as though dragging a weight behind each ankle, sometimes another, his chin up, his whole body expressing pride and disdain. Then he'd spin round, brutal, hulking, using his tie as a whip. IVb, it seemed, were forgotten. But just as Hal was going to protest that it was time they got started Springy turned back into himself and squatted in front of them.

'See?' he said. 'That's how it'd have to be.'

IVb didn't see. What sort of a play was this?

Nothing like a play. No talking.

'Sir,' said a Luddite from the back, 'we all want to be in a play. But how can we? Forty people. Couldn't we each do our own?'

'It was our idea,' chorused the Lollards.

'Quit hollerin'!' roared Springy in his Western Movie voice, tipping an imaginary ten-gallon hat over his nose. Mostly this made the form laugh, and then shut up. It was the only way Springy could keep order. And it worked, on and off, as a way of getting their attention: a chap who could turn himself into a cowboy – maybe knew cowboys personally – was more worth listening to than most.

That first afternoon, Springy made them imagine walking like slaves with chained ankles, wrists bound together. Or act like slave-drivers with imaginary whips. Or strut about, stiff and proud and cruel like slave-owners.

'But sir,' said someone after a while, 'isn't there going to be no speaking?'

'Not much,' said Springy, 'more dancing and singing. Not here,' he added hastily, 'we can rehearse some place – the gym, perhaps. This is only the beginning.'

'How can we all be in one play? – So many?' Betty asked.

'You will see,' answered Springy. 'There will be a need for everyone.'

Fifteen

THERE are times when life passes by with nothing happening. There were months, terms, even, on which Hal could look back without remembering a single special event that stuck out to make one day different from the next. And there are times when too many things happen. The second half of the summer term at Jefferson was one such time.

The first thing to happen was that Mary Malone found out she was going to have a baby. This was not very unusual at Jefferson School, though Mary was amongst the youngest to 'fall', the common term for getting pregnant.

She told Hal and Betty during mid-morning break, after she had had an interview with Campers.

Neither Hal nor Betty could think of anything to say. It's one thing to hear about babies, about sex, and both of them had heard a great deal, in general conversation, as well as in biology lessons. To have it happen to your friend – how different that was!

Mary was standing in the crook of a wall, with her arms outspread along the wall. Her cheeks were puffy, her blue eyes reddened as though with crying. She was not crying now. Her face was sullen, expressionless; it was impossible to guess what she might be feeling.

'Do you get sick?' asked Hal, remembering her own mother. Mary shook her head.

'Are you going to marry him?' was all Betty could think of. At this something of Mary's spirit returned. 'Sure, now,' she tossed back her unbrushed hair, 'and how would I be doing that?'

'Is he too young?' asked Betty.

'How would I know?' Mary frowned, but only for a moment, as though her friend's question was irritating, pointless.

'How can you not know?' This from Hal. After thinking, she continued, 'You're too young to be married, anyway. But you could wait.'

Already her practical nature was trying to make something of Mary's problem. She had been running over all the boys Mary knew. Light broke in her mind: 'Was it – did – how old is Crimp Watson?'

Then Mary tossed her head back, and laughed outright. 'Crimp?' From the tone of her voice the girls knew it wasn't Crimp.

The fact was – and Mary showed no embarrassment in telling them – she didn't know who the baby's father was. 'It could've been several fellers. Sure,' she went on, 'you're as bad as Father Mahy, and me mam and me dad. How am I to tell?'

She heaved herself off the wall and stood with her arms folded about her body. 'They've all been on at me. All but Campers. She just told me what would happen here. I'm to stay on till a few weeks before the baby's born, then come back afterwards to finish at school. She knew I was a Catholic, she said, so there was no use in talking to me. It would all be fixed,' she said.

'Fixed?'

'Where I'm to have the baby. And a little beforehand I'm

to go into a place where they keep you because it will be better for me mam.'

Hal thought of Mary's basement home, already over-crowded. Yes, she supposed it might be better.

'And afterwards,' Mary went on, 'I can stay there, in that Home, until it's adopted.'

Betty began, 'My mother . . . ' she had been going on to say that her mother would have kept her grandchild. Before she could change what she had in mind, Mary said quietly, 'Your mother's gormless.' She turned away and laid her arms on the wall, put her head down and cried.

Betty rubbed her back, gently. Soon Mary looked up, and dried her face with a handful of her long hair.

Betty asked, 'What did Campers say to make you cry?'

Mary sniffed and hiccupped. 'It was what she didn't say. She left me alone.'

'If we understood, we could help,' Hal tried.

'There's nothing to understand,' Mary said, 'only to be left alone.'

For what Campers had understood was that Mary wanted above all to stay at school, not to think about what was going to happen to her. Mary wanted to stay at school because it was better than being at home – a lot better. Always had been. And now more than ever.

Mary didn't cry any more – not ever again, about the baby. The news soon got around. Mary didn't seem to mind people knowing, so long as she didn't have to talk about it, and people soon saw that. To the Lollards she became a kind of mascot, a matter of pride, though they tried not to be too demonstrative, seeing she didn't care for it. Hal didn't know what her own feelings were about Mary and her baby. In spite of talk, in and out of school, and biology lectures about how babies came out, how they got in; in spite of drawings on walls, in spite, even, of her own outspoken knowledgeable references, Hal, deep down, was up against a blank, scared, uncertain feeling: if she could have put it into words she might have said she didn't believe in babies and sex, not for herself anyway. At home the subject never came up. She sensed the depth of her father's fear for her, of what might happen – not just 'having a baby' – but what men could do to a girl. He hated her going out. Kept her on a tight line, always wanting to know where she'd been. As for her mother, Hal remembered her crying when Anda and Bell were born. And the months of sickness beforehand. For her mother, the news of a pregnancy – anyone's pregnancy – was bad news.

Hal was careful not to tell her parents about Mary, and as they led such a cut-off life, hardly seeing friends, avoiding neighbours, they never heard.

On the site Mary's condition gave her importance, set her apart. Crimp Watson, too, gained in stature. He was generally believed to be the father of the baby, and never denied it. Not that there was much talk, after a day or two of curious speculation. For most of the people who used the site, having a baby, whatever words you used to describe the situation, was not so very out of the way: like other misfortunes, it was something that happened to other people, to a friend, perhaps, not to you; but it was not much to be wondered about. Many of the children on the site never heard, or if they did, disbelieved or felt it to be so unreal as not to exist.

Crimp fairly strutted up and down in front of his tower of patched wood, lopsided, but strong enough, and with a ladder that could be drawn up. The roof was on, now, and in the look-out room Mary would lie for hours on a patch of old carpet, eating the food brought to her by Crimp's gang, overlooking on the one hand the site, on the other the canal wall and the canal.

No one except Crimp and his men were ever allowed up, so Betty and Hal had to rely on her descriptions of the luxuries Crimp had provided, the richness of the carpet, the silkiness of the cushions, the food he stole from his kitchen at home.

At school, Springy booked the gym for rehearsals, though this sometimes meant staying late after school. They were to wear P.T. shorts and singlets – he himself turned up in a maroon top and very short sky blue shorts, and lost no time in getting them moving. And at a pace! They were slaves, they were waves, they were a slave-ship; they shuffled in chains, they walked free. Africans taught them to walk with baskets on their heads – a wastepaper basket full of school books – and attempted to teach them their dances. So did the West Indians. Betty Pratt came into her own. Springy had put her in charge of the music. They sang. And at every rehearsal more drums and instruments turned up.

At first all seemed confusion. They danced their own dances, they clapped and sang and beat out the rhythms with hands and feet, sitting on the floor.

'What sort of a play is this?' Dimitri asked after the first rehearsal. 'Aren't we going to have parts? And why no words?'

Many people agreed with him, specially those who fancied themselves as actors.

Springy promised there would be parts 'of a sort'.

'And words to learn, maybe,' he went on, 'but more music,

dancing, rhythm. How many of you here have seen '*West Side Story* – the movie?'

Not many had, for it was old stuff. But Barry began clicking his fingers and the Georgiou brothers, with one or two others, began leaping, spinning in the air, dancing in strange, jerky movements, stopping dead in menacing confrontations, till Springy waved his arms for silence.

'O.K., O.K.!' he shouted, 'you got the message – some of you, anyway. There'll be parts, I promise. But first you have to learn to move.'

' 'T will be a musical!' Mary cried.

'Sort of,' Springy nodded. Then, 'Enough for today.'

After a week or so the play began to take shape. Hal, who refused to play a girl, was to be an African prince. The good-natured Georgious were transformed into brutal overseers. But it was generally agreed that Barry, as a slave-owner, was the best actor among the lot.

'Who'd've thought it?' Mary remarked to Hal in the changing room, after a rehearsal. 'Barry, I mean. The way he can dance and move around.'

'He's much the best,' Betty agreed.

'Yeah,' Hal had to admit, 'the way he gets what Springy's after.' No one was more surprised than she at Barry coming out so strong.

'I s'pose it's all right,' she said as they left the changing room.

'All right? He's real good!' cried Mary. 'Sure and you'd better watch out, Hal Piercy. The way you have him fetching and carrying for you. Didn't I say he was a good-looker? You'll be after losing him if you don't treat him right. If he was my boyfriend . . .'

'He's not,' Hal said quickly and coldly, 'not mine. What

I mean is, all that dancing ... he was supposed to be ill, wasn't he?'

She was thinking of Barry as she had first seen him.

'People get better,' said Betty, looking at her curiously. 'Aren't you pleased he's better? It was you who got him out, wasn't it?'

Somehow Hal wasn't as pleased as she should have been at the success of her plan. It wasn't that she'd liked him the way he was, let alone the way he'd hung around her those first days in the playground. Yet there had been a kind of triumph in his dependence on her. Now he was off, half the time, with the Georgiou boys. Also – though this was a shadowy thought at the back of her mind – she hadn't banked on his being quite so good at anything. This play, for instance. Hal herself wasn't all that good, as she was beginning to find out to her surprise. She moved stiffly, couldn't follow Springy's movements.

'I was thinking,' she said as the three of them reached the school gates, 'maybe he never was ill. Maybe it was all put on.' She didn't really believe this, though she thought he might have been sticking it on a bit.

'That's rubbish,' said Betty, 'remember how he looked that first day?'

' 'Tis all that swimming at the baths with Tim,' Mary looked sidelong, meaningfully at Hal.

Hal jerked her chin up, 'I'm going this way.' She turned abruptly along an alleyway.

The two girls looked after her.

'You shouldn't have said that,' Betty said, 'not the way you spoke.'

'And isn't it obvious she's got a crush on the man?'

'Not a crush. She's serious. She'd marry him if she could.'

Mary laughed scornfully, a little unhappily. 'Who's talking about marriage?'

'Girls like older men.'

'Tim's a creep.'

'You're only saying that because Crimp thinks so.'

'*Crimp!*' Mary opened her mouth as though to sum up her view of Crimp. If she'd been Hal she'd have echoed Miss Camperdown's frequent comment: 'irrelevant!' As it was she shut her mouth as hard as her full quivering lips would allow. 'Aach! men ... aren't you just a kid like the rest? Tim's a drip, I'm telling you.'

It was true that Hal had broken away because of Mary's teasing about Tim. But she also had Barry in mind, remembering an argument she'd overheard between Campers and Springy while she was washing paint brushes in a cubby-hole off the classroom. Springy was predicting that Barry's recovery was too quick to be genuine; Campers had turned on him for interfering 'with his soft, half-baked psychological theories' and she could manage her own kids in her own way, thank you very much. But Hal wasn't sure that Springy was wrong. She sighed, mounting the concrete steps at the entrance to the flats. Barry, it seemed, was still on her back.

She felt tired, all of a sudden. There was too much going on. There had never been a term like it, what with the play at school, and Springy working them as though it was he who was a slave-driver, and the site and the caff – that caff! She wished they'd never started it, and they'd have given up long ago if it hadn't been for the Greek boys being so set on it. And Tim, there was always Tim. Tim, who belonged to everyone on the site, she hardly ever saw him on his own, even. Yet he was always somewhere in her mind.

She found her mother, for once, sitting down. She was in the girls' room by the open window. Anda and Bell were lying on their shared bed, in their panties, keeping cool.

'They're both poorly,' Mrs Piercy said, as Hal pulled her school dress over her head. 'Bell's bin sick. And Anda won't eat. It's the weather maybe.' She looked out across the expanse of dully shining rails, the far-off spread of roofs and chimneys. The sky lay over London like a grey blanket.

Crouching by the window in her pink shirt, Hal looked out too, hoping for a breeze. There was a moment's quietness such as she and her mother hardly ever shared. Hal laid her arms on the warm sill, and rested her head on them. She shut her eyes. She was thinking of Tim, not on the noisy site where dust was kicked up and everyone wanted him at once and there was no place for them to be alone. But lying near a brown pool, with trees hanging down, dipping into the water, like a place she remembered on the Heath. She was thinking, too, of what Mary had said coming out of school, about Barry, how he would go off if she wasn't nicer to him. He was, too – going off more – but not with girls, so far as she had noticed. She never gave him a thought, never needed to. He was just there – for her. But if he went, really went, for good, would she mind?

'How's the caff?' Her mum laid a hand on Hal's hot neck and stroked upwards, moving her fingers through the thick hair.

Hal shivered: she could imagine Tim doing just that. 'I wish we'd never started it,' she sighed, 'there's too much.' Too much going on. Everything was too much: if she'd been Anda or Bell she would have curled up on her mother's knee.

Suddenly she raised her head, staring out over the railway

lines. 'If you – fancy a feller, how d'you know? How d'you know it's real?'

Her mother said, 'Knowing's easy. It's how d'you choose that's difficult.' Mrs Piercy looked out, thinking back, trying to put past feelings into words. 'It's like you're waiting for someone in a car – someone coming to pick you up. One after another they sound their horns, and each time you think – that's him. But it isn't. And then at last a horn sounds, coming round the corner, and you know at once, that's him. And you wonder how you could have been mistaken before.'

'And that was Dad?'

'That was your dad.'

Hal and her mother looked at one another in some surprise: such a talk had never happened between them before. Hal leant forward and kissed her mum on her soft, slack-skinned cheek. This, too, was strange to them both; and Hal was grateful that her mother kept silent, asked no questions.

'I must go,' she pulled on her frayed jeans. She wanted to get away before her father got back and asked about homework.

'I'll have my tea at the caff,' she promised. 'It's going to be great, Mum. Eggs and sausages and that. And the Georgiou boys are keen to do some foreign food. Their dad's going to give them the stuff, and their mum'll show them how to cook it. You must come, some Saturday, you and Dad. Sit out and have tea on the terrace. It's supposed to be opened today, I've just remembered. I've not been to the site for a good few days, because of the play – there's been a lot going on.'

She was away before Mrs Piercy could object.

As she approached the site through the grounds of the Institute – the hole in the wall down the canal had been blocked up – her interest in the caff revived. She hurried past the gardens, where Betty and some younger children were picking peas, a sparse crop in a wobbly row.

'It's our first picking,' cried Betty. 'Here, try one.' And she held out a pod. But Hal shook her head without stopping. She passed the glasshouse with the budgies in it, and the stick insects on their fading branches. These insects gave her the creeps – you couldn't tell them from the twigs. Every so often the glass was broken, and painstakingly replaced. But then everything on the site was liable to be smashed or nicked; it was to be expected. The caff, otherwise, would have been finished earlier; bricks they had snitched, half a sheet of corrugated iron laboriously hauled on the hand-cart from a distant patch of waste land – gone in the night. Most of the stuff was found again somewhere on the site, fought for and recovered. Now the iron roof was securely bolted down, and Hall could see smoke pouring from the iron chimney. The caff was no more than a three-sided shelter, open to a terrace where customers were already seated. As she drew near she saw a board across the open side, brightly painted: 'Hal's Caff'.

Tim was there, sitting outside, and Fred and the other helpers, and a small queue was waiting to be served. As Hal came up, Barry, in a butcher's apron, emerged, holding a tray, balancing it on his fingers like a real waiter.

'Madame!' he cried exaggeratedly, placing the tray in front of Tim, and waving him aside to make room for Hal, much to her embarrassment.

'Shut it! – I'm supposed to be working, aren't I? It's my caff.'

'Not today you aren't!'

Fred reached back, took her wrist and pulled her down

between him and Tim, 'Come on, Hal. This is a celebration. Sit back. You've earned it.' The plank bench was balanced on bricks.

Hal drank tea out of a tin mug. Barry came back with a plateful of sausage and egg, still acting the French waiter, with a scrap of red and white check cotton over his arm. Inside the caff the Greek boys were seen to be shaking a frying pan on the rusty black stove, pouring boiling water from a huge black kettle. Benjie and Kevin were kneeling over a zinc bath, washing up.

Barry, pushing his hair back, watching Hal, dropped his waiter act.

'Like it?' He was smiling all right now, his eyes wide, his sunburnt face alive.

'Sure,' Hal nodded. 'Signboard, too.'

'Put it up last night. As a surprise.'

'And the walls. Whose idea was that, painting them?'

The bricks were painted inside and out, patterned red and yellow and blue.

'I never thought you'd finish it,' Fred said, 'lose interest, didn't I say so, Tim?'

'It was quite a job,' Tim agreed. 'I don't think you'd ever've got the roof on without those sixth-formers from your school coming along one night.'

'It was just an idea, the caff,' said Hal. 'I'd've given it up only Dimitri and Andreas were keen. They said their father'd give them meat to cook.'

She was sitting squashed up against Tim. She had never been so close to him before. The hair on his bare arms was wet, plastered down, this muggy evening, and she could smell his sweat.

'What I like is,' she said, 'it's something real, the caff. Not just a game. It's why we thought of it.'

As Barry whisked past, doing his waiter act, he thought: Hal looks happy. It's what she wanted, the caff; and the signboard – she likes that. For Hal, usually so intent, ready for the next thing, whatever it might be, looked now as Barry had never seen her: dreamy, abstracted, content with the moment. She was smiling as he went by, with all the fullness of her red lips and her white teeth – smiling for him, as Barry thought. But Hal's smile was for no one person, but came from deep inside her.

To his surprise Crimp and one or two of his lot joined the queue. Barry tensed up, expecting trouble. But Crimp had come, it seemed, out of curiosity. Some smaller boys stood aside, yielding place without question, and Barry, to keep the peace, let Crimp shoulder his way to the head of the queue, saying only, 'There's no seats. You'll have to wait.'

Crimp shouted from outside the caff: 'What about the vine leaves?'

'There's sausage – no eggs left,' said Barry. 'Chips?'

But Andreas came out with his frying pan, black inside and out with smoking fat.

'O.K. . . .' he shouted back, 'vine leaves if you want them. Only it'll have to be a special order.' His cheeks shone with sweat and grease, and rivulets ran down either side of his nose.

'You can keep 'em,' Crimp turned away, 'I hate that foreign stuff.' He glowered at Tim. 'Did you know there was blokes all over the place with measuring tapes?'

'They say they're students,' Tim replied. 'They're not

doing any harm. Geography students, surveyors, something of that sort.'

'How did they get in?' Crimp persisted. 'There's some rule, isn't there, *mister?*' (This was one of the ways Crimp showed his contempt – by not accepting Tim as one of themselves). 'No one allowed on the site over eighteen, isn't it? What's their game?'

'It's different.' Fred, with a doubtful look at Tim, got up. 'I mean, if they got a job to do, and this is a place they can practise.'

Nevertheless, Fred, his bare arms tattooed with snakes and bluebirds, went over to take a closer look, and was soon followed by the customers. Before long the caff was deserted, except for Hal and a few helpers, who looked through the hole in the wall that had been a window. It was true: there were about a dozen men, strangers, among the hills and gulleys of the wilder part. One of them set up a tripod.

'What d'they want to go taking photos for?' Benjie asked.

'It's not a camera,' Dimitri explained, 'it's for measuring heights. See? The hill with the clump of trees on it.'

'Well, it's nothing to do with the site,' Andreas was wiping the frying pan with newspaper. 'Tim would've known if it had been.'

'All the same, I don't like it,' Barry said.

He had a go at sloshing dirty knives and plates in the zinc bath, but the water was cold and coated with grease. 'We'll have to do something about this,' he said. Benjie and Kevin had gone off with the others. The Georgious cleaned the knives by thrusting them in and out of the earth and wiping them with newspaper. But the greasy coated tin plates were a problem. And they had to dig a hole to pour the water down. The stove was out, and there was no hot water in the kettle. But the ever-resourceful Georgious meant to keep going.

'We'll take the plates home in the handcart, Mum'll do them. And tomorrow we'll think up something – this was a try-out, the first day.'

They looked round for Hal. But she had gone.

'*Hal's* Caff?' Dimitri jerked a derisive thumb at the sign.

'She liked it,' Barry said, as though that was all that mattered. 'It was real good – you could see what she thought – she'd never believed we'd do it.'

'Well, she'll have to work in it,' Dimitri remarked, wiping a streaky forehead with a filthy wrist.

'Course she will.'

But as Barry walked off home, it struck him: perhaps she wouldn't. It had been her idea, the caff. Now it was actually there she might sheer off, get a new, quite different idea. Barry was beginning to know Hal.

He passed her, standing by Tim, talking to some of the strangers who had appeared so mysteriously on the site.

'G'night!' he called. Hal turned and raised a hand. The way she always did. Barry took the gesture as an acknowledgement, a secret sign between them.

Sixteen

THE night after the opening of the caff, Barry awoke from an uneasy sleep in his hot room under the roof. A light shone in his half-opened eyes, a beam that travelled over the walls, and was extinguished. This was repeated at intervals. When Barry was sure he wasn't imagining it he went to the window. When the light flashed again Barry saw that it came from Crimp's rickety watchtower, black against the furnace-glow of the London sky. Making out that the flashes were some sort of signal, he pulled on jeans and a shirt; he would go down and scout around.

Barry liked the site best at night, and it was not the first time he had stolen out of the house to walk there. Then he regained his old, secret mastery over the place; it became his own country once more.

Barefoot, he crept down through the stale warm air of the stairway well, startled by grunts, sighs and restless movements behind closed doors. Sliding back the bolts of the back door was no problem: he might be any one of the tenants going to the toilet.

Once on the site, skirting the wired-in football pitches, he made his way without difficulty up and down hill through the high dew-drenched grasses and flowers, to the foot of the ladder, which was let down as he approached. Here Barry hesitated: there might be anybody, any intruder lying in wait; it might be death to climb the ladder.

But Crimp's voice, hoarse, peremptory, unmistakable, reassured him. Barry had never been up before. He climbed the ladder, curious to see inside.

'Half a sec.' Crimp shut the door, extinguished the torch and lit a candle. The little room was a patchwork of boarding, and scraps of tarpaulin nailed up to shut in the light. There was a piece of carpet on the sloping floor, benches and a table of sorts, besides a pile of sacks in one corner. (Mary's silken cushions? Barry wondered.)

'I bin signalling for ages,' Crimp said, 'on the chance you weren't asleep, or the light might wake you up. It's a powerful torch.'

'But anyone might've seen.'

'I had to talk to someone – *had* to.'

He was hollow-eyed under his turbulent dark hair, plastered with sweat on his forehead. The heat in the shut-up cabin was unbearable.

Silently amazed at Crimp's appeal, for Crimp had never shown him much friendliness, Barry waited. Something appalling must have happened. He might have killed someone in a fight, not meaning to.

Crimp's next words confirmed his surmise: 'I'm not going home.'

'You can't live here.'

'It was the first place I thought of.'

'What – did you do?'

'It's not what I did. It's my dad. He's bought the site – he and a bastard called Roebuck – he's put up most of the cash.'

'What for?'

'Build flats.'

'But they can't – everyone knows you can't build on the site, else it would've bin used years ago.'

'You can now, or so my dad said. He and some other blokes were talking downstairs. There's a corner in my room where a bit of piping goes down into the lounge. You only have to put your ear to it. I often listen. When he's bin giving me funny looks – means he's planning something he knows I won't stand for – butters me up, gives me a present.'

'Mary said he beat you.'

'That too. But presents are worse. Belting doesn't mean much except he's in a foul temper. It's over. But presents ...'

Barry tried to take in the life these two led. It was difficult to imagine; but he was beginning to see why Crimp behaved the way he did, and to feel some sympathy for him.

Crimp went on, 'An air rifle it was tonight, so I knew it must be something big. Truth is, I thought it might be to do with a bird who's bin around. I've heard them talking.'

He suddenly thrust his neck forward like a cockerel to take a closer look at Barry. 'Cripes! Never thought of it till now. What's your other name – queer name, innit? Unusual.'

Barry cut across Crimp's ramblings (he'd have to get out soon, the lack of air was making him feel faint). 'The site, you were saying they've found they can build on it after all. How come? What about the tunnels underneath?'

'They can now. It's bin gone into and proved. Lighter construction – ways of building – and far fewer trains. Lots of them tunnels aren't used.'

Barry remembered the friendly strangers on the site, the measuring tapes and the instruments: 'It's called a theodolite, son.' They'd been close – wouldn't say what they were there for.

'The Council?'

The Council it seemed, had been squared. The adventure playground was to be allowed to continue as far as it had been cleared, in addition to a piece of land belonging to the Institute.

'And even then not for ever.' Crimp was twisting and untwisting a length of rope as he spoke, flexing his strong wrists. What he had to say didn't come out easily, but in jerks prompted by Barry. 'Not if it upsets the plushy bastards in the new flats. They've only just got planning permission. I heard them talking tonight.'

'Does Tim know?'

'I reckon no one knows yet, and what'll *he* be able to do?'

Barry noted Crimp's contempt. 'Why've you got it in for Tim? I've never understood.'

'No special reason. He's a creep. I hate creeps. We could've done without him.'

'We could *not*! It was his idea – the playground. We'd never have got it without him.'

'He's a drip. You could knock him down easy. Fred now – he'd have you on your back as soon as look at you.'

'He never has!'

'Point is, he could. Tim – he's all talk. I hate talk. "Reasonableness"!' Crimp filled the word with disgust. 'That's grown-up talk, garbage. Give 'em what they want, make the kids think they're running things, while all the time they're ready to crack down. Sell you down the river.'

'Not on the site – not Tim.'

Crimp smiled in his ugly way. It wasn't his fault he had teeth like his father's; but it increased Barry's distaste, as Crimp went on, 'Tim specially. What's it all come to, his talk? He's bin treated like a kid, same as the rest of us. And he won't be able to do a thing about it – you'll see.'

Barry shifted a leg; he was beginning to get sleepy. But Crimp continued, 'Another thing – his not doing proper work. Who'd leave off being a scientist to work with a bunch of kids?'

'It's just temporary.'

'And his smarmy way of letting the girls get sweet on him? How d'you like that?'

'He can't help it, I s'pose, if they do.'

'Hal? *Your girlfriend?*'

Barry went cold, then hotter than ever. 'You're round the twist,' he said, not caring if Crimp went for him. Not that he believed what Crimp had just said. But the very idea was a shock to him.

Crimp pressed on, 'I'd soon stop Mary...'

A silence fell. For Mary, both boys recognized, had gone beyond being 'sweet' on grown-ups. She had, in a way, become a grown-up herself without meaning to.

'What did you get me up here *for?*' Barry asked harshly.

'I told you – I needed to talk to someone. Besides, you get ideas. You might think of something.'

Barry, impressed that Crimp had noticed him that much, liked him better. He said, 'I can't think of anything now. You said yourself there's nothing we can do. We've had it, the site, except for the bit we can still use. I'm going to bed. Think of school tomorrow.'

'I don't go to school, at least, not a proper school.'

'What sort of school?'

'A crammer. To get chaps into posh boarding schools, like what Dad's got planned for me. I don't mind.' Crimp sounded as if he did.

Desperate, now, to get back to bed, Barry said, 'Use your loaf – you'll have to go home, may as well now. Maybe they've found out already.'

'I'll nick a boat and go down the canal sooner.'

'He'll leather you?'

'Not half he wouldn't. But it's not that I mind. It's his getting the site, the dirty tyke, worming away.'

Barry was surprised at Crimp's feeling for the site – he'd been so aloof, not joined in anything except the five-a-sides. Barry said as much.

Crimp kicked the table so that a leg collapsed. ''Tisn't the site. It's Dad getting it, having his way, building all them classy flats.'

'Anyway,' Barry tried to find the clumsy door fastening, 'I'm off.'

But Crimp gripped his wrist, 'Here's an idea,' he said, hoarsely, urgently. 'How about some of us climbing down the ventilation shaft – there's an iron ladder runs down inside as far as you can see.'

'You really are round the twist,' Barry said, trying to free himself.

'We could get down there and prove it – don't you see? If the place really *is* lousy with tunnels, even if they're not used – even *more* if they're not used – we could prove it was dangerous. All get together. Make a stink, get in the papers.'

Barry sensed that Crimp was beginning to enjoy himself, and that made him all the keener to get back to bed.

But Crimp still held his wrist. 'I bin thinking,' he said with a croaky laugh, 'we'll be related, sort of.'

'What d'you mean?'

'Didn't you know? Your name's Padgitt, isn't it? You didn't know about your mum and my dad? She's the bird he's bin going out with.'

Crimp loosened his hold, and Barry slid down, slumped against the wall.

'You didn't know?' Crimp squatted beside Barry.

With difficulty, Barry fetched his breath. 'She had a feller – I guessed that. She's bin out a lot lately. She's on her own a lot. But –'

He had a very clear picture of Crimp's father. The idea of him and his mum ... And then Crimp had said something more. 'What did you mean, about us being – related?'

'She wants him to marry her. Been to our place a lot lately. Mind you, Dad's not so keen. You can hear that.'

Barry pictured Crimp's ear pressed to the pipe in his room. He said, 'It's funny, though, them meeting.'

'Known each other before, it seems. Or did once years ago. As I say, she's keen. And he's coming round to it. He won't have you, though. That's what they bin on about, mostly. It's enough, he says, having me around. But I'm going to school. So are you, aren't you?'

Barry was speechless, remembering all that had passed between him and his mother, the school – the lot.

'There'd be holidays,' he said at last, considering the prospect of sharing a house with Crimp.

'Part of our holidays'd have to be spent with them. But I got an uncle in the country. And there's holiday camps and places. They got it all worked out. I reckon she was scared to tell you. Or wanted to wait till she was sure.'

'I didn't give her much chance,' Barry said, feeling in the face of Crimp a strange loyalty to his mum. 'It'll be day soon,' he said, as Crimp dowsed the light and the door creaked open. There was a misty lightness in the sky behind the chimneys.

The air after the cabin was cool enough to make Barry shiver. As he moved among the summer flowers and grasses that soaked him with dew to the waist, stumbling over roots, into bushes, he had no thoughts in his head. He wanted to sleep.

Seventeen

THAT same morning Barry got to school somehow, mindful of Campers' threat to send him away if he didn't attend regularly. He felt stunned; the whole day passed without his being able to think back to his dream-like experience in Crimp's hideout. He could eat no dinner, and fell asleep during afternoon lessons. Miss Camperdown, after asking if there was anything the matter – he shook his head – sent him home early. He lay down and slept.

When he woke the full shock of Crimp's revelation broke upon him. His mum and Crimp's dad! There were moments when he hoped it might not be true. But there seemed no reason why it shouldn't be. He couldn't ask her; he would have to wait till she told him. Maybe she had meant to. In fairness he had to admit that she had tried. There had been times, lately, when she had begun to speak, with a look of puzzlement and sadness mixed with a tone of resentment and complaint that filled him with dread. Cranmere College loomed up, and he wouldn't stay to hear what she had to say.

'You know I only want what's best for you,' she might begin; and he would dash out, down to the site, before she could finish.

One thing: he wasn't waiting around tonight till she came home. From his window he could see smoke rising from the chimney in Hal's caff and he hurried down.

Dimitri waved a fish-slice at him, 'What was the matter at at school? You O.K. now?'

Barry nodded and began to load up a tray with mugs of tea and plates. Customers were already ranged along the benches on the terrace. But he couldn't attend, couldn't remember the orders.

Hal, furious, got him in a corner. 'If there's anything wrong, say so!' But Barry couldn't answer. Hal snatched the tray and turned her back on him.

But at that instant something happened which emptied the caff of customers and staff – Kevin ran up shouting that Tim wanted everyone double quick down by the recreation hut.

Tim, Fred and other helpers stood together near the hut. They stood silent, waiting, while from every part of the site people gathered – from the five-a-side pitches, Benjie with the ball under his arm, from the little hills and valleys in the wild part, children leaving their crazy lean-to's, the swing-rope on the tall sycamore, the new tree-walk. More slowly the gardeners laid down their tools, Betty giving a hand each to Anda and Bell. Only Crimp, Mary and his gang stayed away in their look-out hut.

Tim got up on a bench. He looked very white. He held up a hand for silence, and for once everyone took notice and was quiet.

'There's bad news,' he said without preamble, 'rotten news.'

The site, he told them, was to be closed. It was to be sold. There was nothing he – anybody – could do.

Immediately there was an uproar. Tim waited. Then Fred got up and shouted for silence, waving towards the Institute.

Two men were approaching, Crimp Watson's father leading. Tim said, 'Here's the man who's bought the site. He wants to talk to you.'

For the first time Barry saw what Crimp had seen – maybe Tim was a bit wet, hopeless, too easily resigned, however angry he might feel inside.

Crimp's dad, all smiles, spoke cheerfully, persuasively. Somehow, he made people listen. He almost made his hearers feel he was on their side, a benefactor wanting the best for everyone.

'Houses are needed,' he cried, 'flats – I don't have to tell you that.'

It was Hal who shouted, 'Flats for rich people!' And many voices echoed her, a rising tide of anger. Mr Watson waited. When the clamour died down he continued: 'Ah – just wait a bit. There's a gentleman here from the Council who has something to say about *that*. But first I'm making a pledge to you – my word on this: we're going to keep what we can of the playground. You won't lose out – that's my solemn pledge.'

There was a perplexed murmur, while the councillor changed places, being helped, somewhat shakily, by Fred, on to the bench. What he had to say didn't interest his hearers, and his explanation that Mr Watson's firm owned other land, far more suitable for council flats, which they were letting the Council have in exchange for the Bute Street Site, was heard in silence, sulky, menacing. The councillor was keen to get away; but a boy shouted, 'Hey, mister! What about our playground?'

Mr Watson shook hands with the councillor, hurried him off, and answered for him in his jolly positive way, 'Right, lad – we'll walk round and take a look. The gardens to start with – and a very fine show indeed, if I may say so. The budgies and the animals and all – they'll be untouched, being on Institute ground. Now for the five-a-sides ...' A sizeable crowd followed, out of curiosity.

'Very nice,' Mr Watson's smile almost cut his face open as he patted the wire mesh round the pitches. 'Very decently done. Sport – that's what we want to encourage in you youngsters – I just wish I'd had your chances.'

The old brick ventilator was to be scrapped. 'Ventilation – we do these things differently now.'

'What about Hal's caff?' cried Benjie, waving towards the slope. Black smoke still streamed from the chimney.

'Well, no!' Mr Watson never stopped grinning. 'Looks like an old steamer, doesn't it?' There were one or two sniggers from people who thought Hal and her lot were cocky. 'No. All that part will have to be levelled.' He walked on. 'But we might make room for some nice swings and so on, here.'

Hal wasn't there. She had stayed with Tim and was sitting on the table in the recreation hut, along with one or two others.

'What will you do?' she asked.

'Nothing I *can* do. Fred and I – all of us – have been up half the night talking. We only heard late on – after a Council meeting approving the sale. No, there's nothing. As long as the site couldn't be built on we could have it. Now it can be, no argument.'

He rubbed his face with his hands and pushed his hair back in a gesture Hal had come to know and, like every aspect of Tim's being, treasure in memory. 'There's not a thing,' he said.

'We'll stop it somehow,' said Hal. 'Start an Action Group.

Banners and protests – march through the streets – leaflets and all.'

One of the helpers broke in, 'No use, Hal. Not if it suits the Council. They want more land for building. No stopping it.'

'Course we will,' cried Hal, 'you wait!'

She felt dashed by Tim's lack of enthusiasm.

'The worst thing is,' he said, 'I've let you all down. It was my idea.'

'Nurts! It was a good idea, and it worked. It's not your fault. What I meant was, what are you going to do when the site closes? Go and be a play-leader somewhere else?' Her tummy tightened painfully at the idea of his departure.

'I'm going back to work at the Institute, probably. I had to stop my research because the money ran out. But someone has offered to back us. Some city chap. At least, his firm is putting up the money. Man called Roebuck.'

Barry came in in time to hear Tim's last words; but it wasn't till later that the name struck him – Roebuck, Roebuck! The man seemed to be everywhere. But he didn't think about it then, because of seeing Hal sitting on the table by Tim, half-turned towards him, intent, her head turned on her long, beautiful neck that Barry so often wanted to touch, to hold, to stroke gently. Not looking at Tim, he left the hut. Another thing Crimp had been right about, Tim and Hal.

Outside were the Georgiou boys, still wearing their butchers' aprons.

'You can take those off!' Barry laughed grimly.

'Why? Hal's caff hasn't been bull-dozed yet. Who's to stop us?'

Andreas reminded them. 'But we gotta go now – remember? Springy wants us for a late rehearsal.'

Untying his apron Dimitri glanced at Barry. 'You look terrible. Bet you haven't eaten anything all day. Come on home with us – there'll just be time to get something from Mama.'

On the way the boys got it out of Barry, how his mum was going to re-marry and how he was having to go away to school and perhaps for the holidays as well. Just telling them made the idea less unbearable. But it also made it more real – more likely.

'We'll have to think of something,' said Dimitri. And his brother, nodding across Barry, agreed. 'Yes. We have to think, but it will take time. How much time have you got?'

Barry laughed. 'It's Mum's marrying, not me – I dunno!'

'She's afraid to tell you? Or not sure, perhaps?'

'Scared, I should say, the way you look sometimes. No, really.'

Andreas made a face, pulling his eyes into slits, dragging the corners of his mouth down till the lips disappeared.

'Shut it!' Barry, not really angry, elbowed his friend into the gutter; and the three of them ended up in an amicable skirmish on the pavement.

Mrs Georgiou's kitchen was dark and warm, and full of smells, rich and varied, of cooking which, at his first visit, had put Barry off; but now they were familiar, and he sat down hungrily to bean salad, olives, cheese, soup and bread with seeds on it.

The family had eaten, and their father sat back, his hands clasped across his tummy, wearing a vest, his braces trailing over his pin-striped trousers, a glass of wine at his elbow.

His wife was small and olive-skinned, dressed as always in black, with a small gold cross on a chain and tiny gold earrings. The rhythm of her movements comforted Barry, smoothed away the raw edges of the day.

Through the open door growing herbs and flowers mingled with the cooking smells; in the yard, beyond the butcher's van, there was a square of grass, and plants growing up the wall, and the beginnings of an arbour with a vine trailing over it.

Mrs Georgiou turned dark-ringed brown eyes on him; her lined face crinkled into a smile. 'This your first meal today?'

Barry, licking a cake dripping with honey, admitted that it was.

'His mother is marrying again – a bad man,' Dimitri began to explain, but his brother kicked him under the table and said loudly, 'He is sad because his chick is sweet on someone else.'

Barry was scarlet. Everyone looked his way.

Mrs Georgiou spoke sharply. 'That is enough. You are too young to know about such things. Nor do we speak about them. At home you would not dare to speak so, in front of your parents.' She appealed to her husband for support.

But he only shrugged his shoulders, reminding her, 'We are not at home now. Here everything is talked about. And children do not respect their parents.'

Andreas began, 'It's not that we don't respect you, Mama. But we want ...' He was afraid of hurting her by saying: We want to be English boys now.

Encouraged by his father, Dimitri said, 'Hal isn't a chick, anyway. She is very beautiful, but –' He felt he was getting into deep waters.

'It is she who will be sad soon.' Andreas, turning to his

father, explained, 'Hal is sweet on Tim, you know, the guy we told you about who runs the playground. But Tim doesn't notice her, of course.'

Mrs Georgiou's indignation brought her to her feet again. 'That would be very wrong, with so many in his care – like a schoolmaster.'

'But naturally.' Both boys were eager to speak, and one said, 'Lots of girls are sweet on Tim. But he wouldn't notice them even if' (he looked rather nervously at his mother) 'even if he was a baby-snatcher. He's got a girlfriend of his own.'

This news gave Barry quite a lift. 'How d'you know?'

'Saw them together down by the canal. Not close to, but it was Tim all right. I only saw the girl's back, and I think I've seen her before. One of the helpers, probably. Couple of days ago.'

Dimitri got up and reminded the others about Springy's rehearsal. No one wanted to move. And Mrs Georgiou protested that it was too late.

'Never mind, Mama. Only a week or so and you shall come to see us, Andreas and I, beating the lights out of the others. And Barry here – oho! Barry – he is truly horrible! We have whips.'

'What sort of a play is this for children?' lamented their mother as the three tumbled out into the yard.

'A fine play,' Dimitri called back, 'for you too Papa. Lovely girls!'

'We shouldn't tease Mama so. She can't understand.'

'She must learn.'

Turning to Barry, Andreas said, 'All that about you and Hal. I'm sorry. But I had to say something quickly – it was important to stop Dimitri telling about your mum, how she might be getting married. It would have been too soon. I told you, we must make a plan.'

Barry thought to himself that he had not much minded the talk about Hal. He couldn't imagine getting really worked up about anything in the Georgiou household. It was like living in a family in another land.

Eighteen

WHEN Barry brought back an invitation for Open Day at Jefferson, he didn't really expect his mother to come. She and Barry, recently, had seen as little of one another as possible – polite but distant, wary, both of them. Mrs Padgitt had stopped railing at her son; and he had tried to avoid arousing her exasperation.

She stuck the invitation in her mirror.

That evening when Barry came in late, he was surprised to see a light under his mother's door: she wasn't usually in when he got back, or else she was asleep – he no longer went into her room to see.

She came out, holding an envelope. 'Take this to school tomorrow, will you?'

'What is it?' Barry, nervous as a shying horse, avoided taking the letter, instantly fearing that it referred to his leaving.

'What d'you think? R.S.V.P., it said. I'm going to get off work early – can't get there before six, but that'll be all right?'

'You mean you're coming to our Open Day?' Along with surprise and suspicion, Barry felt a spark of pleasure.

'It's right I should, isn't it? I thought you'd be pleased.'

She was looking up at him – for he had grown taller than her – and he saw nothing in her face but uncertainty, a hope of pleasing him. He nodded, and kissed her.

'I thought I'd wear my blue – well, bluey-green it is, the one trimmed with velvet. It'd be just about right, I thought. Not too dressy, but smart, good looking.' She was at her best, lit up, talking about clothes.

'You always dress right, Mum. You know that.'

Just for that evening the gap that had widened between them closed; they felt comfortable and ordinary together while they had a cup of tea, and Barry tried to tell his mother something of what to expect, though not much for, as he said, 'Jefferson's different. The play, for instance, I couldn't explain it to you, not in words. It's a sort of musical,' he said, remembering Mary Malone's remark.

'I shall like that,' Mrs Padgitt stirred her tea. 'I like a nice musical. Plenty of songs and dancing?'

'It's difficult to explain. No one's ever seen anything like it. My part – it's quite a big one. But you wait. Yes, lots of singing and dancing,' he added after consideration, for though he didn't mean what she meant, it was true enough.

Open Day was at its height when Mrs Padgitt came through the iron gates. The asphalt playground that swept round the school on three sides was full of children and grown-ups. There were stalls selling a variety of goods, an acrobatics display, and several bands – like a fairground. The noise was terrific.

Barry and some of his friends were sitting on the steps up to the front door, watching out for their relatives and remarking on newcomers.

'Now she's *really* smart.' Betty Pratt drew Mary Malone's attention to Mrs Padgitt, hesitantly making her way through the crowds. 'See? That greeny-blue dress – see how it fits. And not too obvious. Just right for today.'

'My mum,' Barry happily admitted.

'You're not looking bad yourself,' Mary eyed his new maroon T-shirt and cinnamon-coloured jeans of the latest cut, his smoothly styled shoulder-length hair. Nothing did more for Barry's self-confidence than to have Mary eyeing him up and down in her appraising way. 'Put on weight,' she commented, 'lost your stoop. I told Hal you were a good-looker. Didn't I, Betty? That first day. You were a bit of a weed.'

'You saw possibilities,' Betty agreed. Barry didn't mind being talked about; he only wished Hal had been there to hear.

He ran down the steps, waved, Mrs Padgitt spotted him and seemed relieved.

'You look real good,' he said, taking her arm. She did, too, except he wished she didn't have to wear a petal hat. But this seemed a popular form of headgear, and at least hers matched.

Mrs Padgitt, responding to the unusual, almost joyful expression on his face, allowed herself a gentle squeeze on his arm as they mounted the steps.

Barry had reason to look joyful: the Georgiou brothers had just told him they had fixed it with their mum for him to come and stop with them if the worst happened: he could stay on at Jefferson whatever his mum's plans were.

'So,' Andreas had cried, thumping Barry on the back, 'you can say goodbye to those underpants and socks and the blazer with the crest on it and the masters (he crossed his arms and looked wooden like schoolmasters in a photograph) and the chapel – poof!' In a gesture he blew up the chapel, and Cranmere College went up into thin air.

'That school,' Dimitri gave a shout of laughter, 'is one big joke in our family. You see, first Andreas said, very serious, that we both wanted to go to such a school, and about the healthy cold baths, and the prefects and much beating and running before breakfast, and so on.'

'It was a big tease,' put in his brother, 'you know we are always teasing Mama, and she never knows whether to believe us.'

'But it was serious, in the end. She cried. How could we want to leave home? And anyway she could not believe even England had such terrible schools, and so on.'

'So when we told her about you, and that there was such a school, it was not difficult to make her see that you couldn't go whatever happened.'

'Papa wasn't so easy. But, in some things, he does what Mama says. Now, when we annoy him, he threatens to send us off to Cranmere.'

'You must come to supper soon and you will see what a big joke the school is with us. We only have to say, "Mama, where are my new underpants and socks?" and Papa goes off. Choked himself the other night.'

'It was Hal's idea – she put it to us. But at first we didn't see how we could. You'll have to sleep on the floor.'

'We'll take it in turns.'

'I don't mind,' Barry spoke anxiously, 'so long as it's O.K. It's settled?'

He was reassured that it was.

With this news under his belt, Barry was free to feel genuine affection for his mother. For he was free: the threatening shadow of the new school which had fallen on them both was lifted. As to the rest – her possible marriage – he had only Crimp's unreliable word to go on. His happiness left no room for vague forebodings or the possibility that his mother might not see their plan as a happy solution. These might come later; but not now.

The Georgiou boys waiting on the steps bowed over Mrs Padgitt's hand so charmingly that she gave them a sharp look; but seeing they were foreign, she took no offence. Indeed, by the time they had all reached IVb classroom their good looks, their sleek black hair, combined with the faint smell of a classy brand of cologne, persuaded her, as she remarked to Barry when she had a chance, that they seemed suitable friends, better than she'd expected. She looked round the room, half-full of parents and children.

Miss Camperdown introduced herself, her clear voice audible above the buzz of talk, 'Have you seen Barry's paintings?' With a nod she sent the boys off and drew Mrs Padgitt to a quiet space near the huge window that made Mrs Padgitt giddy to look through.

'You'd like to know how he's getting on? Of course you would. As I'm sure you know, he shows promise.'

She waited a moment in case Barry's mother wanted to ask anything.

'I always knew he was bright,' she said cautiously.

Hal, pinning up some drawings that had fallen down near by strained to hear what they were saying, and heard some of it.

'Of course he has difficulties. You might like to come and talk to the school doctor next term. After all,' Miss Camperdown smiled, 'you know him so much better than we do.'

'I don't, you know.' Mrs Padgitt's rush of long-pent-up anxiety, overcoming her caution, was clearly audible from where Hal stood. 'I don't know him at all, not since his illness, though he's long got over that. No, it's that playground that started it. He's not my Barry, not like he used to be.

Why, he used to depend on me ever so, a real bind it was sometimes being on me own with him. I couldn't get out, hardly.'

At this point Campers detected Hal leaning towards them and gave her a meaning look which sent Hal off to find her own parents.

Barry showed his mother everything, not that she was likely to remember much what with all the goings-on, the puppet shows, the chemistry experiments, the gymnastics. They had tea in the Domestic Science room, served by Mary Malone. 'At least she's English,' Barry's mother remarked.

'Irish,' Barry corrected her.

'You know what I mean – so far all your friends seem – well, foreign.' By this Mrs Padgitt meant black, Greek, the lot. 'Not that I've anything against –'

'Mum,' Barry breathed a warning, 'we've had all that out. Just keep off it while we're here – yeah?'

The petals on Mrs Padgitt's hat quivered a little as she ate her chocolate éclair daintily with a plastic fork. But she was set on avoiding trouble.

Wishing to please, she remarked to Mary who came round to fill up her cup that the éclairs were very good. 'Made by you girls, you said?'

'Sure, and by the boys, too. Lots of boys come to Domestic.'

'Well ...' Barry's mother, he could tell, was becoming more than ever bewildered by this extraordinary school.

She looked after Mary in her starched smock, produced by Miss Camperdown. 'Now, *she's* a nice girl – real nice. You could bring her home to tea.'

Barry smiled that thin-lipped curly smile which never failed to make his mother uneasy. What had she said now?

She was relieved when the time came for the school plays to begin.

The plays took place in a hall used for scientific and other demonstrations, with a steeply raked auditorium, so that spectators looked down on the stage, bare except for an arrangement of blocks and steps which could be arranged according to need. There was no curtain, but an elaborate battery of lights.

The house lights were dimmed, the stage gradually illumined, and the show began, each class performing its chosen entertainment.

IVb was to come last after the coffee interval.

No one who saw the play was able, afterwards, to say very much about it. Some were struck by one aspect, some by another. That it was about slaves and slavery, this much was clear. But as the spectacle – for you could hardly call it a play in the accepted sense – progressed, much that had seemed clear became unclear, complicated.

At its beginning the house lights were dimmed; the stage, too, was in total darkness. The sound of African drums was heard, faint, then louder with the dawning of light, a red, sultry glow. The steps had been drawn together at the back of the stage to form a smaller stage with graduated steps. Here stood three figures, silhouetted against the backcloth, then, as light increased, the chief among them was recognizable as Hal, wearing a leopard skin and a jewelled headband. (Benjie's resounding: 'She's an African prince!' was hastily shushed.) She seemed to be scanning the horizon.

From the wings the Georgiou boys swaggered on, stripped to the waist, wearing – like all the cast – jeans, and with whips wound like snakes about their wrists. They were (there was a flutter as programmes were consulted) sailors, slave-traders. Hal welcomed them, clapping her hands to summon dancers to entertain them. Other instruments, wind and stringed, joined the congo drums.

Hal clapped her hands again; the dancers retreated. Light dimmed to blood-red, and there was silence except for the drums' changed rhythm, allied now to a new sound, the clink of metal, terrible as its meaning became clear.

For now, from the back of the hall (every head turned), a line of prisoners slowly descended, bowed, moving as though shackled, bound wrist to wrist. The drummers so drew their palms across their drumskins as to express the dragging pain.

Downstage the Georgiou boys waited, one each side where there were steps up from the auditorium, their rhinohide whips uncoiled, whipping the boards as the slaves mounted the steps, keeping the inexorable beat, watching as the slaves were led into a concentric, maze-like pattern which, when completed, and when every man and woman had lain stretched out, pressed together, was seen to form the exact shape of a ship's deck.

The clink and the footbeats were stilled.

Audible in the sudden silence, Hal's father whispered, 'That is how it was. That is how the slaves were packed, deck on deck, without an inch of space wasted; like fish in a tin. That is the truth.'

Gradually the red, torrid light dimmed, changed to sea-green light; and now, against muted drums, a gentle sound was heard, like a quiet breeze in the rigging of a ship. Everyone in the cast took part, humming a sea-shanty, a farewell without hope of return.

Light faded to darkness, and a slight movement ran through the audience as they shifted, tension released.

Dark figures could be heard moving stealthily about the

stage, which, with little delay, was flooded with brilliant light.

There, on the top step, stood Barry, in a ruffled shirt open to the waist. And grouped round him were ladies, girls with sashes and flowers in their hair. The scene was a Caribbean island, and Barry a rich slave-owner. Every West Indian in the audience recognized the background music.

Barry made the audience laugh with his affected foppish gestures as he took snuff, accepted an imaginary cup of chocolate, and smiled in the most horrid way on his ladies, who swayed elegantly, fanned themselves and crooned their admiration.

Before this exalted group the slaves appeared, driven by the Georgiou boys, ferociously beating the boards with their leather thongs. And against the light-hearted song of the planters another, grimmer, music played in harsh counterpoint as the slaves were whipped across the stage cutting sugar canes, their step marked by the clink and beat of drums.

The Georgiou boys were not wholly sinister; they cringed at a gesture from their master, the slave-owner, clowned and chased and fell over one another in haste to obey; and turned somersaults (which they were good at and had insisted on bringing into the act) in mock fear.

The audience laughed, as they were meant to; again the tension was broken as it was becoming unbearable.

Now the tempo of the play changed abruptly and confusingly, as the slaves turned about, cast off their imaginary chains, chased Barry and his ladies off the stage, and began to dance and sing to the accompaniment of a steel band.

As suddenly, the stage was given over to African dancers; then the two, Africans and West Indians, mingled together, threading their way in and out with enough precision to show that what they did had been carefully rehearsed. Upstage on the steps Barry, the Georgious and others, stripped to the waist, were leaping, spinning and clicking in Springy's special kind of dancing – its relevance was not clear, but it expressed the spirit of the whole.

The beat was irresistible: confusion, exact meaning became unimportant. The audience, who had begun to stamp and clap, now rose to its feet; those who knew the tunes sang them, and many who didn't sang just the same – sang whatever came into their heads. At a pre-arranged moment Barry flung out his arms: instantly the dance stopped, noise ceased, the musicians collapsed over their instruments. The play was over!

The cast bowed where they stood, bowed and bowed again. But the audience were not satisfied till they had called 'producer!' and 'director!' so often that the exhausted players at last understood that Springy was being called for and boys ran off to bring him in. This took time, for he had to be tracked down to the staff toilet, where Campers was putting wet cloths on his head, assuring him the play wasn't going to turn out the disaster he had feared.

Cheering, they carried him on, the cast parting to make space downstage.

'Springy!' shouted everyone as he was set down, and, 'Speech!'

But he shook his head, still draped with a wet cloth, and could only smile and spread out his hands, and clasp the nearest members of his cast to him in an indiscriminate gesture, indicating they were all in it together, for better for worse, and now it was time to go home.

Nineteen

FOR a day or two after the play no one from IVb felt like going to the site. Apart from the general feeling of flatness that follows such an event, there was much clearing-up to be done, not only in connection with Open Day but, more urgently, arrears of homework to be made up, 'revision' for end-of-term tests.

Hal even found a kind of relief in resuming her evening prep at the kitchen table, with her dad opposite, and her mum quietly moving about clearing up. It was like coming back home from a world outside where, as she had expressed it, 'too much was happening'. The weather continued grey and sultry, and the oppressive heat was at its worst towards evening, but their high flat, with doors and windows open, was cooler than anywhere else.

Her parents had made it clear that they had been impressed with Open Day; even her father, who was hard to satisfy, found little to criticize, if it were not that the play, in his opinion, was unsuitable for children.

'It was true,' he had said. 'All of it was true. People need to know, *ought* to be told how things were. But it was not for children.'

Her mum said quietly. 'They are not children. Not any longer. I keep on telling you.'

'What are they?' He turned his gold-rimmed glasses

severely on his wife. 'You're not telling me our Hal here is a grown woman? Or that boy – the slave-owner. A boy playing a man. Yes,' he interrupted Hal's impatient exclamation, 'of course it was only a play. And the part suited him. He is clever, that boy, but cruel. No, the trouble with kids today is that they play-act all the time – play at being grown-up.'

Mrs Piercy stood over him. 'Don't you start now – you make me sick the way you talk sometimes. If you'd play with them more when they *are* kids, and watch 'em grow up, you'd see what they're like – a darn sight better than we were, when they've been brought up right, like our Hal has.'

And Hal burst out, 'And if it's Barry you meant, he's *not* cruel. Trouble is he's too soft – he used to get set on. Only he's learning. He's just a super actor – couldn't you see that?'

Her dad removed his glasses and looked at her. 'At home,' he said, 'you're a child. Remember that when you go out.' He continued to look at her and Hal guessed he was thinking how skinny she was, and how her small breasts still didn't show through her blouse. Not like Mary and Betty and other girls of her age. This shamed her, and her father's awareness made her the more self-conscious.

Hal's mum came round and put her arm on her shoulder: 'Enough of that, Clem, Hal's a good girl. And she's growing fast. In her mind, too. Let her be.'

But Hal wouldn't be let alone. She wanted her father to say more about the play. 'Why was it bad for us, the play – go on, Dad, why was it good for you but bad for us?'

Her mother said, 'I know why. I'll tell you some time.'

After her father had gone to sleep, Mrs Piercy answered Hal's question. 'The play upset him. It made him cry.'

Hal looked at her mum, and saw that it was true. She had never thought of her dad crying. Men didn't.

'When? I mean, what part of the play? The slaves in the ship?'

'No. After, when they sang "Shenandoah".'

And Hal went to bed without getting an answer as to why a play which made people cry could be good for grown-ups but bad for the kids who had made it.

The Piercys didn't refer again to Open Day or the play. It wasn't their way to get involved in discussions, let alone protracted arguments. For the most part, Clem Piercy had the last word.

But Hal had begun to have a new feeling about her mum; that in some way they understood one another, were on the same side.

More than anyone else except Campers, she sensed, her mother understood how difficult things were sometimes, and getting worse; how she longed for the day when she could be properly grown-up, and not, as she felt now, neither one thing nor the other.

A day or so later, she was sitting at tea with the family. Only Benjie was absent; and he burst in, ignoring his dad's 'You're late!' Leaning over the table he gasped, 'Barry says you're to come *now*. It's the site!'

Hal jumped up, swallowing a mouthful of chips, washing them down with tea as she made for the door followed by Benjie. But Clem Piercy shot out an arm and caught him: 'What is all this? Who is this man?'

'He's not a man,' Benjie tried to wriggle free, 'he's Hal's boyfriend.'

Mr Piercy swung round to question his wife, 'You know about this?'

'That Hal has a boyfriend? No. But is it surprising?' Hal could see she was pleased.

Her husband frowned, 'And we know nothing of him?'

'If he was the boy who was so good in the play, we talked to him – in the interval, wasn't it?'

Hal nodded. And when her father turned back to her, 'Is this true?' she answered curtly, 'Yes.'

Now she had admitted it to herself. Barry was her boy-friend. And her dad could say what he liked about it.

Highly entertained by this new turn of events, her mother said, 'You'd best be going. He's in a hurry, it seems. No, Benjie, not you. Your tea's in the oven, no going out till you've had it.'

Mother and daughter exchanged a look of complicity as Hal got out while the going was good.

At the site she saw that a strong fence of linked wire had been put up, cutting off three-quarters of the area. What they were left with was a strip of land running parallel with the wall at the bottom of Barry's garden, wide enough to take in the five-a-side pitches, and leaving room for the conventional swings that Mr Watson had promised, near the recreation hut at the Institute end. Beyond the hut were the Institute grounds, outside his newly acquired property. At intervals along the wire notices had been erected: 'Trespassers will be prosecuted. Warning. GUARD DOGS ON PATROL.'

Beyond the wire Hal's Caff stood on its hillock. No smoke rose from the chimney. And in the far corner by the canal wall Crimp's look-out tower stuck up against the sky like a crooked finger.

A small crowd were pressed against the fence. Looking. There was nothing more they could do, except kick a ball around the five-a-side pitches as some boys were doing.

Barry came to meet her.

'How long ...?' she began, ready to blame him, to blame anyone.

'When I came back from school this evening.'

The Action Group, thought Hal, the marches, the leaflets – she'd had the ideas; she'd done nothing. So no one else had.

'It was that school play,' she said, 'took me mind off.'

'We couldn't've stopped it – no one could've.'

'Tim would. Where is Tim?'

'Gone off to see the man from the Council. Says he wasn't given proper notice. Never seen him so wild.'

Dimitri, near by, put in: 'It was the dogs – the notice about the guard dogs. He was mad anyway. But when he saw them ...'

Hal and Barry leant against the fence like the others. To the north and west the sky cleared; the westering sun slanted along the site; a freak wind shook the trees, turned back the leaves in waves, shivered the grasses, and the late summer flowers, yellow and purple, bearing smells of sunburnt grass, trodden earth and the all-pervading privet flowers with their end-of-summer-term scent.

Bushes bent this way and that revealing and covering in their rank growth paths hard-baked by drought and bare feet. Then all was still; waiting, so Barry sensed. Waiting for the rightful owners to come back. In spite of the bare patches, for all they had made it their own with wood and twisted metal, rubber tyres, all the scavengings from a derelict neighbourhood, the site had never looked wilder, more deserted.

'Let's go back,' he said to Hal, 'not now, but tonight.'

Hal looked at him to see if he meant it.

'Come back,' he urged, 'after they're all asleep in the flat.

We'll lie up on that hill there – with the three little trees. I've often been up there when it was too hot to sleep.'

They both looked at the notice-boards.

'I don't believe it about the dogs,' Hal said.

'It's meant to scare us.'

'We'll soon know, anyway,' she giggled uneasily. Then, 'Have you really – bin up there at night?'

He nodded.

'O.K. I'll come if I can get away. Not for the whole night, I couldn't. But I might for a bit.'

'Meet you at the Institute gate. Some time after ten. You'll have to climb over.'

'Can't say when, exactly.'

'Doesn't matter. I'll wait.'

They both figured out the distance between the Institute gate and Barry's little hill, crowned with the three young mountain ashes. It would make some distance to cover unseen.

'We'll think of something,' Barry said confidently. This was the kind of adventure that Hal had been waiting for all her life, without knowing it. That Barry was the one to dream it up no longer surprised her. 'You may be cooky, but you have fab ideas!'

'And he's not the only one!' The Georgiou boys had come up in time to hear her last remark. 'Cooky! – bonkers, I should say!'

Hal turned, 'Who?'

'Crimp Watson. Did you know he's up in his look-out tower? Says he's not coming down – got enough food and water to last a week.'

'How d'you know?'

'Mary Malone. She's in the gardens with Betty, crying fit

to bust, 'cause Crimp wouldn't let her up. She thinks his father will kill him.'

'Crimp's got an air-gun.'

The news of Crimp's siege had spread, and people were crowding along the wire fence. But there was nothing, no movement to be seen from the hideout. Boards had been nailed up inside the windows. The ladder was drawn up.

The silence that lay over the site was tense, expectant, like the stillness before thunder.

Then the storm broke – or so it seemed. But the rumble came not from the skies but from the Institute. With a splintering of wood, a crumbling of bricks, a machine came lumbering on to the site, leaving the too-narrow entrance in ruins behind. Gathering speed, it roared across the site, levelling every obstacle in its path. It was about the length of a Diesel railway engine, manned by two men in yellow crash helmets. The machine was painted bright yellow, and on the side in huge black letters: 'ROEBUCK AND WATSON, EARTHMOVERS.'

'Where's Tim?' cried Hal, running as she had never run before – perhaps Tim would be back in the shed. 'Tim, Tim!' she cried, as though she could be heard above the noise.

Tim was there; he had come running out of the hut, followed (later, Hal was to remember with amazement) by Campers.

The machine had stopped within a yard or so of the brick ventilator, as though considering whether to butt into it then and there. Instead, the two drivers contented themselves with circling round once or twice, enveloped in a cloud of black dust, then nosed around the borders of the wilder, hillier part, making wild skirmishes into the privets, tossing earth and bushes sky-high. At length, with a rock and a lurch the earthmover turned about and made straight for the rise topped by Hal's Caff and the sturdy sycamore with the swing rope on it.

'They'll tip over!' cried Barry as the thing charged at the slope.

Tim shook his head. 'They'll level it,' he said, putting his arm round Hal's shoulder, 'it's good practice ground.'

And in a very few turns, unbelievably it seemed that they had. As though satisfied, they drove off towards the gate, where the machine finally came to a halt.

When the dust had settled a little, the watchers could see what had happened to Hal's Caff. The whole of that part had been levelled, leaving only a scattering of unrecognizable débris.

'I can see part of the stove.' Dimitri, drawing his wrist across his eyes, unashamedly snivelled, from rage as well as loss.

'We can't be sure,' said his brother, 'it could be anything.'

Behind them Campers' clear voice shook with anger. 'I've been in the gardens. Some of the smaller kids are terrified out of their wits.'

Betty came up with her brother and Mary Malone. Anda and Bell ran crying to Barry and Hal.

'The woman who runs the gardens is there with them. The young ones without brothers or sisters here – I think we ought to get them home somehow. She says they ripped off the back of the shed where they kept the rabbits – the brutes! Because the entrance wasn't quite wide enough.'

'It's like films of World War One,' someone remarked in a low, shocked voice.

Dimitri began: 'I see now why Crimp...'

'Stuff it!' His brother trod on his foot.

Everyone understood that Crimp's whereabouts must be concealed from the grown-ups.

'Crimp!' Kevin exclaimed. 'Was that his dad, then – him and Mr Roebuck – on the earthmover?'

'It's called a scraper,' remarked some know-all in the crowd.

'As though we cared,' Andreas silenced him.

And Mary Malone cried out with bitter passion, 'You think the bosses soil their hands? Them's the Micks. Wild they was, couldn't you see it? 'Tis us they get in to do their dirty work for them. Micks, they call us. Is it drunk and wild we are? And why shouldn't we be –'

'Shut up, Mary,' said Campers, gently but conclusively. 'Come and help me get some of the young kids in my car – those that haven't anyone to take them home. Hal, you can take care of Bell and Anda. Betty can take some. And Tim – you've got the pick-up?'

Anda, on Barry's shoulder, sobbed, 'The budgies is gone!'

'No,' Barry answered her, 'they're coming back. See?'

And there they were, circling above the broken glass-house.

'I'll bring Anda,' he said. And as the party trailed along the fence, he whispered to Hal, 'Our hill – it's still there. You'll come, just the same?'

Hal looked at him in amazement, half-admiringly. 'You really *are* round the twist. After all this?' She gestured towards the devastated plain. Towards the canal the little hill still stood, the three mountain ashes and the deep grasses.

'Just *because* of that. Hal, please. Tomorrow the hill will be gone. I've thought – it would be best if you come to my place. We can get through the house easy. I'll watch for you coming.'

'Through your mum's bedroom window?' she said mockingly.

'She may not be there. Anyhow – leave my mum. I'll – I'll sit on the steps if necessary, or come to the corner.'

'Then I s'pose I'll have to,' said Hal. 'But I'm not promising. I've got to get out of the flat, remember?'

Twenty

BARRY carried Bell almost all the way to the flats. He had to wake her up, and she wailed as she was put down.

'You'll come?' he reminded Hal. 'I'll wait all night if I have to.'

'I said I'd try.' The intensity of his expression gave her a cold jumpy feeling. Perhaps he really *was* seriously 'unbalanced', as Springy seemed to think. Ever since the play he'd been different. As though he could do anything he wanted. Whereas before he'd had to be egged on to try things. Cocky, Mary had called him, and he hadn't minded, only laughed. He went about snapping his fingers as though the dancing had never stopped in his mind.

The Georgious thought his behaviour funny; they encouraged him. But Hal was uncertain.

Such thoughts drifted through her head as she toiled up the flights of stone stairs (the lift being stuck as usual), carrying Bell, dragging Anda by the hand. The nearer she got to home, the more unreal Barry's plan seemed.

Trailing along the empty, echoing gallery, Hal saw her mum at the door. Her finger was on her mouth, 'Come quietly,' she whispered, 'your dad's asleep, went off dead, he did, soon after tea.'

'He shouldn't have to go so far to work,' Hal whispered back. But what was the use? He was afraid of losing his job.

When Anda and Bell had had their dresses stripped off and were laid asleep side by side, Hal tiptoed back to the kitchen.

'Was he very mad after I left?' she asked, taking a mug of cocoa her mother offered her.

'He went on a bit. About your boyfriend.' She smiled, and the tired lines round her eyes crinkled. Hal was relieved that she was pleased at the idea, but she herself must have looked uncertain, for Mrs Piercy asked quickly, 'He's a good boy?'

'Oh yeah. He's all right. We're just friends, you know, Mum. We aren't ... I mean we don't – he's not like some of the others.'

'Drink your cocoa.' Mrs Piercy could see Hal was troubled. 'Well then?' she waited.

'It's just that Barry ... It's since the play. You remember how he was at first? Dead quiet – I told you – when he first come on the site. And then at school?'

Mrs Piercy nodded, trying to keep awake; not that she didn't care, but she was dead on her feet, swaying with exhaustion.

'Since the play he's been different. Always acting up, showing off. You can imagine Campers has been on to him, even Springy – it's as if he couldn't stop, slow down – I dunno.' Hal sighed. Barry, it seemed, was still something of a responsibility, whether she wanted it or not.

'That's nothing,' her mother, relieved, took the mug and rinsed it out. 'He's above himself, that's all. Your dad was right, in a way, that play you did, it got you all wound up – all of you. *You've* not been yourself, neither.'

She turned the mug upside down on the draining board. 'He'll come down to earth with a bump.' She yawned.

'You go off to bed, Mum. I'll lay up for the morning.'

'About time,' said her mother, kissing her. It was the first time she could ever remember Hal offering to help without having to be asked. 'You're growing up fast,' she said.

When Hal had put out the things for breakfast, she hesitated. She sat down, eating a slice of bread and jam. She glanced at the clock on the dresser. It was after ten. She wouldn't go, of course. She thought of the little hill and the rowan trees.

'Tomorrow they'll be gone,' Barry had said.

She went through to the bedroom. Anda was snoring. The room smelt stale and sweaty. Hal pushed open the window and leant out. The night was dark, the scene below brilliant by contrast. Under arc lights trains shunted, an express train glided out of a tunnel, a long freight train, in the opposite direction, gathered speed, hooted. The railway always seemed more active, more exciting, by night.

Hal had never felt less like sleeping. And Barry? Would he really be waiting? Standing, perhaps, at the corner by the tobacconist's? He was crazy enough, she ruminated, he might just be. She pictured him standing there, dawn coming up, shivering. 'Nurts!' she cried soundlessly, and flung herself on her creaking bed. But in five minutes she was up again, rummaging in a heap of clothes on the floor, feeling for a sweater.

The front door made the tiniest click as she shut it behind her. Her rubber-soled sneakers, as she tiptoed down the balcony, were soundless.

Once in the street, she began to run, then, pulled up by the thud of her feet on the pavement, slowed to a walk. Now all she was afraid of was that some policeman would ask her what she was doing, up so late, and alone. But there were still plenty of people about, once she left the silent deserted streets waiting to be pulled down.

Pubs were beginning to empty, though men and women still stood about in the warm air smoking, with glasses in their hands. Shops, warehouses, empty houses with smashed windows, the smell of the lino factory, of blistering paint, rotting vegetables – all were familiar, yet transformed by night, unfamiliar.

She hurried as best she could without risking notice, being asked questions. And if Barry wasn't there? Well, she wasn't sorry to be out – she could get home easily. Just padding through the streets, no one knowing where she was, made her heady with rebellious excitement.

Barry was leaning against the rails, just where he'd said he might be. Seeing him was something of a shock. Hal, she now realized, hadn't expected him – Barry, who, less than two months ago, couldn't get out of the house! Just for that – for it had been her doing – she could have hugged him. She strolled up casually. He had seen her; he waited; when she came up he took her hand. He was trembling a little.

'Cold?' she asked. 'Sorry you had to wait.'

He shook his head. Hand in hand, without speaking, they came to his door. He made a noise opening it, but didn't seem to notice her warning hand on his arm. He led her through the hot, sick-smelling passage, down two steps, so fast that she nearly stumbled: 'Steady on!' she hissed. But he already had the back door open, they were crossing the yard, past the stink of the toilet, down the garden, over the wall.

In the ditch the other side, they stopped. She could hear his uneven breathing.

'What's the hurry?' she whispered, and put her hand on his chest with a touch of her old anxiety. 'Get your breath back, do.' She felt his heart pounding through his sweater. 'You're not scared?'

'Course not!'

She giggled: 'Well, I am, a bit!' She took his hand and held it to her chest. 'Wouldn't be fun if we weren't.'

'No need,' he said, 'I bin watching. There's a couple of blokes on the site. They patrol the fence. But mostly they stay in the recreation hut. No dogs.'

'But that was when it was light?'

Without answering, he drew her along the wire fence. 'We can get over easy. Here – where there's a post.'

In a minute or so they had dropped down. They were on the site. There was no moon. But under the glowing London sky it wasn't difficult to make their way, snaking through the thick scrub, up to the hill, waist-deep in dew-drenched grass and tall flowers.

At the top, under the branches, Barry dropped down, hugging his knees to his chest. 'We've made it!' he said, still whispering, but more in wonder than from caution.

Hal sat down, her heart still pounding. 'It's all right,' she said, 'but what if we had to get back? It's miles to the fence.'

'No one will look for us here. Why should they? If the guards come out at all, it'll just be to walk along the fence, and round by the Institute. I watched 'em. They're lazy sods. There to protect the machinery, the stuff they've got already for tomorrow.'

'Tomorrow,' Hal remembered. Tomorrow the earth-movers would finish the job they'd begun.

'Let's not talk about tomorrow. Let's not talk.'

Barry lay flat on his back, one arm behind his head, the other at his side. Hal lay stretched beside him. Their arms touched, and Barry felt for her hand.

But he couldn't keep silent. 'I used to watch you.'

'Yeah – you said.' Hal didn't want to remember the Game. But she couldn't help adding, in case *he* was remembering it. 'It was a kid's game.'

'I know. I'll tell you something, I used to call you "The Indian Queen".'

'Why ever?'

'It was how you looked.'

Hal said nothing.

'And sometimes you turned into a cheetah.'

'A what?'

'The most beautiful animal in the jungle – and the fastest.' When she stayed silent, he continued, 'I used to think how we'd go through the jungle – at night – after the place was empty.'

'And come up here?'

'And come up here.'

They gazed up at the sky through the leaves. 'It's like grape bloom,' he said.

'Like what?'

'Grape bloom. You know – grapes aren't shiny. I had a lot in hospital.'

The serrated leaves over their heads moved a little in the breeze.

'Soon it will be dawn,' he said.

For some time Hal had been wondering if Barry would kiss her. She had been kissed before; but she hadn't much enjoyed it, wet, hurting, clumsy, down in the bushes. Barry, she thought, would know how to kiss her. At last she said, 'What are we going to do now?'

His hand tightened on hers. 'Just stay here. Isn't that enough?'

She turned on her side towards him.

'We aren't kids,' he said, in a strange, hard voice, 'we aren't playing games.'

Then Hal knew he had guessed about the games they had played in the bushes – games they were too old to play.

'We're not kids,' she said in a small uncertain voice, 'but we aren't grown-up, either. I hate it. It gets worse.'

'What gets worse?'

'Oh, I dunno. People.' She thought of her dad. 'They don't know what to expect. And yet they expect more. Campers, now.' Suddenly she sat up. 'Campers!' she exclaimed. 'Her being there today. Why ever? I never thought till this moment!'

'You really didn't?'

'There was so much happening. It seemed – well, not surprising her turning up. I dunno why – I never give it a thought.'

'You mean you don't know?'

Hal thought. 'I didn't. But I do now.' She put her head on her knees. Campers and Tim. How could she not have known?

'They had a row. She was mad at Tim for giving up his proper work and running the site. And now they're back together. Something like that. I thought you'd be sure to know.'

'Did you suppose Tim would tell me?' Hal spoke bitterly. 'How d'you know, anyway?'

'Mrs Georgiou told the boys. *She* heard because it's her uncle owns the caff – the one we went to when we met Campers.'

For what seemed a long time, Hal sat with her face pressed down on her knees. Campers and Tim. The two people who mattered most in the world. It was a double betrayal.

Barry put his arm around her shoulder, and it was firm and strong, not trembling. 'D'you mind so much?'

When Hal didn't answer, he went on, 'You just said we aren't kids any more. Having a crush on Tim, well, half the girls did. Nothing to it. But your minding him and Campers – that's real kid's stuff. You must've known he'd have a girl-friend – who better than Campers?'

'It *wasn't* just a crush. He *did* like me – it was something special. Remember that first day?'

'Course he liked you. If it hadn't bin for you backing him the playground idea would never've got off the ground, more'n likely. He relied on you a lot.'

Forgetting where they were, they had begun to talk in raised voices.

Without warning, a voice said behind them: '*Shut up!*'

Hal and Barry froze. A figure ghosted out of the bushes, close enough to whisper urgently: 'For Christ's sake! Don't you know they've got dogs?' It was Crimp.

'Dogs?' Barry whispered. 'They never. I bin watching. Men. But no dogs.'

'A feller come on the site just as it was getting dark. A bloody great Alsatian police dog on a chain – went once round the site, then took him in the hut.'

They could see the hut from where they sat. A shaft of light showed as the door was opened.

'Hold it!' Crimp grabbed Hal's arm as she and Barry jumped up. 'Don't try getting back – you'll never make it. Come up with me.'

Barry saw the sense of it. 'Right, then. You first, Crimp, Hal next.'

Without another word or a backward look Hal followed Crimp, snaking through the bushes as once they had done playing the Game. But now it was real. She caught the sound of men's voices, and a dog barked. But a long way off.

Crimp, who had stopped to listen, whispered, 'They're just starting on their rounds. They'll follow along the fence – where you got over, that's where the dog'll pick up your scent.'

Off he went again, with Hal at his heels, never thinking to look back, sure that Barry was close behind.

But at the foot of Crimp's ladder she turned. 'Where's Barry?'

'He'll be here in a sec – get up the ladder.'

'Not without Barry.'

'Don't be a damn fool – he was just behind you wasn't he? Get up – and hurry!'

Crimp smacked her on the rump like a reluctant calf and she licked up the shaky rungs and through the door. Within, all was darkness.

Crimp stood at the foot of the ladder, waiting.

Twenty-One

WHAT Crimp said about the men patrolling the fence had made Barry pause, waiting till the others had gone ahead. Then, without stopping to think, he doubled back on their track. His one idea was to get between Hal and the dog. But as he ran down the arched, leafy, scratchy tunnels, bent double to avoid swishing the branches, it came to him that he might get to the wire fence and the post they'd used to climb over before the security patrol reached the spot. If they were only making a routine patrol they might be leisurely – according to Crimp they were a lazy lot. They'd see him, of course, but there was a chance he might vault the fence before the dog got there. Even – though this was a slim hope – reach the safety of his own garden wall. Maybe, having spotted the trespasser, seen him safely off the premises, they'd leave it at that.

Now Barry had reached the edge of the brush. Before him lay an open stretch of ground, between him and the fence. He gathered all his strength for the sprint. But even as he broke cover, the dog saw him, barked furiously, and dragged his dog-handler at a run towards Barry. Barry reached the fence and the post with the dog on his heels.

'Stay where you are!' shouted one of the men. 'Keep still and he won't hurt you. But if you move . . .'

Barry turned, his back pressed against the concrete post.

The great animal sprang to the limit of its chain, pinning Barry to the fence with a paw on each shoulder, its teeth and tongue and panting throat within an inch or so of Barry's face.

At an order, the dog dropped to the ground and lay crouched, ready to spring. A second guard came forward and took Barry's arm in a strong grip: 'Any more of you coming?'

Barry shook his head.

'We'll wait a bit,' suggested the guard with the dog.

They waited, listening. After a while they took Barry back to the hut. The strong light after the darkness hurt his eyes. He was pushed into a chair in front of a table littered with beer cans and cigarette packets. A man sat down opposite, reached for a full can, stripped off the closure and poured it down his throat, keeping an eye on his prisoner the while. Up till now Barry had been too shocked to react. But now the full force of the shock, the memory of the dog springing, came over him and he started to shake. When the dog-handler, sitting near the door, gave his dog a biscuit and the animal moved, Barry jumped.

'He's only a kid,' the dog-handler said; he sounded disappointed.

'What of it?' said a third man sitting in a corner. 'Nine times out of ten it's kids do the damage.'

The man at the table suddenly leaned forward. 'And what was *you* up to – eh? Come clean, now. What was you after?'

'N – nothing,' Barry answered. He would have given anything not to sound scared.

The man thrust his face close. 'I asked you what you was after.'

'I was just lying up on the hill,' Barry said. 'The one with the trees on it.'

The man in the corner stirred, 'That's a likely one, I don't think – chuck us a can, Bill.'

The dog-handler with the dog's chain still wrapped round his wrist moved, and the dog at his feet growled. Barry gripped the table's edge. The heat in the hut was stifling, his ears buzzed and he put his head down on the table.

'He's fainted.'

'Shamming,' said the man in the corner. He came up behind, seized Barry's hair and jerked his head upright. He sloshed some beer over the boy's face.

'Waste o' good liquor,' remarked the dog's master, and he, too, after telling his dog to 'sit', joined the others standing round Barry. 'Shan't get much out of him,' he commented. 'Just the same,' he suddenly shouted, 'you was trespassing. Saw the notices? Don't deny it!'

Barry shook his head. The three were like fishermen looking down on a very small fish, considering how to make the most of it.

'Trespassing,' repeated the man at the table. He had begun to fill in a form under his fist. 'Name? Address?'

Barry, in a whisper, told him both.

'Better check,' said the dog-handler. 'I'll go with him.'

They yanked Barry to his feet, but it was clear that he could hardly stand. 'I'll take the van,' the man said, '*and* the dog,' he added with a sour look at Barry. The dog was put in the back, and Barry sat in front.

The light was on in Mrs Padgitt's room, and in a matter of seconds after the guard's four knocks, loud enough to wake half the street, she flung open the front door.

Oh, dear!' she cried, seeing the man holding Barry's arm.

'What's 'e done? What's 'e bin up to? Whatever it is, officer, you may be sure 'e was led into it.'

She grabbed Barry's free arm, and the man let him go.

'Trespassing, ma'am. Serious offence – on the Bute Street Site.'

'And what about the others? You're not just going to pick on him, surely?'

The man looked at Barry. 'Says 'e was on 'is own – never saw any signs there were others.'

'You won't be charging him then? He's never bin in trouble before.'

'I'm not a police officer. It'll be reported to the owners of the site tomorrow – Roebuck and Watson. It's up to them to prefer charges.'

'Not a police officer?' There was a change in Mrs Padgitt's voice. 'Roebuck and Watson, you say?' She was almost haughty. 'Well, you won't be wanting anything more from him tonight. Thanks for bringing him home.'

'Up with you,' she said, closing the front door. Light from the open door of their rooms at the top of the house filtered down the well of the staircase. Enough light to show Barry doors on every landing being closed ahead of them. One lodger in his dressing-gown waited to see them go by.

'Police?'

'Not police,' Mrs Padgitt swept by in her swirling nylon négligée. 'Thanking *you*, Mr Bowser. Just a friend, seeing Barry home.'

'Some friend,' grumbled the old man, 'knocking fit to wake the dead.'

Clearly he didn't believe Mrs Padgitt.

'Nor will anyone else,' she said, once their door was closed behind them. 'That was a policeman's knock if ever there was one. But you shan't be took up – shamed. I'll see to that. Whatever you was up to.'

She seemed very sure of herself. Barry stretched out on his bed, empty with exhaustion and the fear he had been through.

His mother came close, sat down on the bed, leaning over him, putting her face close to his in a way she hadn't done for months.

'What *was* you up to – you and your little gang of toughs? Burning the hut? Stealing tools? Don't tell me you *wasn't* led into this. I've bin waiting for something like this to happen.'

He lay with eyes closed.

'You're all in!' His mother pulled off his jeans and sneakers and pulled the bedclothes over him. 'I'll get you a drink. Nasty tough louts! Whatever they let you into, it's the last time, I swear. They're not right for you, son, brought up so careful. The College vacancy's still open – Mrs Roebuck'll see to that. And I got everything ready. The police'll be kept out of it. I'll ring Mr Watson first thing.'

There was a pause while she filled a glass with water from the landing tap.

He propped himself on an elbow to drink it.

Her voice when she spoke again was hesitant, even a little embarrassed. 'You didn't know I knew Frank Watson, did you? Childhood sweethearts, you might say. I bin meaning to tell you, only there's never bin a chance, the way you've bin coming and going.'

With an effort, Barry lifted his eyelids to look at her. 'I know, Mum. I know about Mr Watson.'

He handed her back the glass, lay down and turned his back to her.

There was nothing more he could do.

Twenty-Two

NEXT morning, Hal was later for school than she had ever been before. She missed the first period altogether, and it was a piece of luck for her that Campers was taking the second. One look at Hal's face was enough. This and her stammered: 'Sorry, miss. Overslept,' without further explanation. Clearly something serious had occurred at home. With a nod she dismissed Hal to her place, guessing that Hal would talk to her in her own good time.

At break Hal came to her.

'It's Barry, Miss. We don't know what happened to him.'

'I noticed he wasn't at school.'

Hal put her face in her hands, swaying on her feet from anguish and lack of sleep.

Campers put an arm round her and made her sit down. Hal came out with the whole story, till the moment when, 'Crimp waited at the bottom of the ladder. We thought he was just behind us, so he waited, ready to pull up the ladder as soon as Barry was up.'

There was a pause. Hal went on, speaking with difficulty, 'Oh, miss! – we heard the dog. And men shouting. Over by the fence. Somehow he must've gone back. They got him. There wasn't anything we could do.'

Later Crimp had helped her over the canal wall near his

look-out tower. She had got home and into bed without waking anyone up.

'I'll call round after school and see his mother. There may not be much I can do; but I could find out a bit more. And Hal,' she continued as the girl turned away, 'nothing very terrible will happen to Barry. I don't know much, but nothing serious, I should say.'

'It was the dog, Miss. Like a wolf it sounded.'

'Why don't you go home for the rest of the day? Have a proper sleep.'

But Hal shook her head. Her parents would come asking questions.

'Then I think you should go to the sick-room. I'll give you a note for Sister.'

Hal had told Betty and Mary because she hoped Mary might be able to find out more. Mary had a way of communicating with Crimp. He would let down a carrier bag on the canal wall, and they'd exchange notes and she'd put in bottles of water. Sometimes she'd put food in, but not often unless he gave her the money.

'I can't understand his father,' Betty said. 'You'd think he'd have the police out looking for him. Boys can't just run away – disappear – like Crimp did two days ago.'

'Crimp thinks his dad knows where he is. He's not troubling himself, he's going to wait till they bulldoze the place. Then Crimp'll have to come out. He thinks he's punishing him more, Crimp reckons, leaving him up there to sweat it out.'

The two girls fetched Hal out of the sick-room when school was over, suggesting they should go down to the site to see whatever was to be seen. They found quite a bunch of Jefferson kids, and others, too, who had once been in Hal's gang, staring moodily across the wire fence. Only a few irrepressible footballers, Kevin and Benjie among them, were using the pitches.

The rest were there to see the monster machine finish its work. But Hal never took her eyes off the window in Barry's room.

'He ought never to've turned back like that,' she repeated over and over. 'Or maybe he couldn't keep up. I ought to've looked back.'

But the Georgiou boys guessed the truth. 'He went back because of you. To give you time to get to Crimp's place. And once they'd got him, it was enough. They never came looking for you two?'

She shook her head. 'We waited ages. But no one come after they took Barry.'

She turned away. Her shoulders shook and she wept, hanging on to the concrete post.

Both boys put their arms round her, telling her Barry was the bravest boy they had ever heard of, not to be cried about, but to be proud of.

'Wait till we tell the family!' exclaimed Andreas. 'They will be honoured that he should stay with us.'

Even as they spoke, a cry reached them from Crimp's watch-tower. He was signalling frantically, pointing to Barry's window.

Barry stood there motionless behind the glass, helpless, like a wax model, worse, like the living model he had been long ago. Then without a sign, he disappeared.

'The blazer!' cried Andreas. And from his brother, 'Oh, help! The tie!'

Two things happened at once. The scraper started up with a roar, making straight for the little hill where Barry and

Hal had lain. At the same time Crimp, not waiting to let down the ladder, shinned down a post, ran straight across the site in the path of the monster, sprinting across open ground.

With a bound he leapt the fence, and with a hoarse, wordless battle-cry scaled Barry's wall. Hal followed, and the Georgious, and in an instant boys and girls were pouring over the wall, through the back door and up the stairs.

Hal and Crimp hurled themselves against Barry's door, but there was no need. The door swung open. The room was empty.

'In here!' Hal cried. But Mrs Padgitt's room was empty too. Empty until it filled up with boys and girls, some not knowing why they had followed.

'Look,' Hal said, leaning out of the window. A taxi was disappearing round the corner.

'It is finished,' cried Dimitri, his fists beating the window-sill till tears flowed.

'I don't know,' Crimp said. 'That car – it's turning round. It's following the taxi!'

For the taxi had nearly collided with a small car, recklessly driven. The car came on, slowed down as though the driver was uncertain, then turned in a wild swoop, bumping over two pavements and disappearing in the wake of the taxi.

'They are detectives,' said Dimitri. 'They've seen Barry is being kidnapped.'

'It's Campers,' Andreas cried, 'and Tim's with her!'

While Hal and her friends stood looking down on the deserted street, the crowded room began to empty, as room was made for people to return down the stairs, like seeds running through a funnel. What had happened was that Fred and two other helpers from the playground, seeing the disturbance, had hared along to the garden and the back door, where they found a number of children jam-packed in the basement passage. This was quickly dealt with, the children dispersed, leaving room for the rest to come down.

'What was it?' one asked another. And a third answered, 'Something's happened to Barry Padgitt.'

They had all heard Crimp's rallying cry, and one followed another. In the same way, urged back by Fred's shouts, they returned to the strip of land that was all that was left of their playground. Here they stood about in dispirited groups, some drifted away, or stayed to watch the gigantic depredations of the scraper, which, having made short work of Barry's hill, now turned towards the furthermost corner of the site, and Crimp's watch-tower up against the canal wall.

Hal, the Georgious and Crimp went through to Barry's bedroom in time to see the wooden structure smashed up, pieces flying high into the air. It was an awkward corner, and part of the canal wall was damaged before the machine was satisfied, reversed, and nosed away leaving a neat level stretch.

Hal couldn't make out from Crimp's set, expressionless face how much he minded the destruction. Mary will mind, she thought. She asked, 'What will you do now?'

Crimp shrugged, rocked on his heels, his thumbs thrust into the waistband of his jeans.

'What will you do?' she asked again, feeling a new concern for Crimp because of what he had done to help her and Barry.

'Go home. Where else?'

'Your Dad – will he leather you?'

'Yeah – most likely.' Crimp sounded indifferent. 'But I don't suppose he'll say much. Never does.' He gave her a sharp look, 'I'm not his kid, y'know. That's why he doesn't like having me around. I'm glad I'm not his kid.' He was looking at her intently to see if she believed him; it was important that she should.

'But you're –' Hal stopped. She had begun to say, you're so like him to look at, but refrained lest it be hurtful.

In fact the idea had just come to Crimp. And why should it not be true? He could hardly remember his mother. He didn't blame her (though he often had done) for running out on him, seeing what his dad was like. But if he could think of himself as her son, not his dad's, a lot of things would be easier. He would be really free, not having to think of that twister as his dad. He could be sure of not growing up like him.

Fred looked in. 'What're you doing in here? Thought we'd cleared out the lot of you. Right plague you are. I've bin trying to pacify the inmates – scared rigid, the old 'uns are. I'll have to see the landlord, if he can be traced. Otherwise you won't even have what's left of the playground. You there,' he turned to Crimp Watson, 'you can get out right now. I'm in charge – shall be when Tim officially leaves – and I'm not having trouble-makers.'

'I'm leaving anyway.'

'Are you really staying on?' Hal asked Fred when Crimp had gone. 'I should have thought it was all over.'

'They'll want someone as play-leader. There's the pitches and the Institute gardens and activities in the recreation hut. Can't let kids down.' He sounded almost apologetic, as despondent as everyone else. 'Let's go.' He led the way downstairs.

On the site diggers were already scooping up and carrying away piles of earth and debris. As they passed the fence a scrap of thistledown was blown over; a small piece of life from the place that had been their own had survived destruction. Hal caught it.

'Crimp was right,' mourned Dimitri. 'It's all over – finished. And poor Barry – he is finished too. When we tell Mama . . .'

Twenty-Three

'IT is finished,' Dimitri had lamented, meaning more than the playground that lay flattened before them, black dust still coiling in the air and settling in the wake of the departing earthmovers. He was speaking, too, of Barry.

That evening, after telling his family at supper about what had happened, he said it again, 'It is finished.'

The family sat silent for a while, saddened, for it was indeed a sad story that the boys had told.

But Mr Georgiou said that they had yet to learn that nothing in life is ever 'finished'.

'Life,' he said, leaning forward to fill his glass, his chair creaking under his weight, 'is like a road that turns and twists and rises and falls so that no man can foresee what lies ahead. Sometimes a bend will open up new country. Sometimes we are brought up short by a sign saying: "No Road". But then we see that the way lies to the right or left. So it will be with Barry. As with us all,' he said, remembering how they had left their home in Cyprus.

None of them could have foreseen the surprise that lay in store for them all – that in less than a fortnight Barry himself would be sitting in this very place, with Hal beside him!

No one at Jefferson had heard anything more about him, except that Campers had told Hal that he had gone away for a few days with his mother. The events of that night and the following day had been a severe shock. He wouldn't be returning to school for the final week. As to his future, she refused to be drawn. 'But I can tell you he won't be going to that College,' she said with a smile, 'so cheer up, Hal, and tuck into some food. You must've lost weight over this. Things'll turn out all right for Barry, you'll see.'

'That's what I said, miss – that you'd somehow make things all right.'

'You expect too much, Hal. Things can hardly ever be made "all right". But sometimes they sort themselves out, with other people's help. His mother, for instance.'

'His mum?' Hal's wide eyes showed her disbelief.

'Yes. Who better? She needed help – more than Barry, really.'

That was all Miss Camperdown would say.

But Hal cheered up, to the relief of her friends, and now, at the beginning of the summer holidays, here was Barry, staying the night with the Georgious. His mother had been here earlier, to have a talk with Mrs Georgiou, for he was after all to live with them during term-time, and keep on going to Jefferson.

Andreas and Dimitri had been to Hal's flat to tell her the news, and bring her back to supper which they were eating in the garden, where there was just room for a table and benches under the vine that Mr Georgiou was training to grow overhead.

Hal couldn't wait to ask, 'What happened after you left in the taxi? That *was* Campers, wasn't it in the car behind – and Tim?'

Mrs Georgiou was bringing out a dish of beans and a mixture of cold vegetables dressed with oil and vinegar.

'He should not be tormented with questions now,' Mrs Georgiou interrupted, 'wait till you have eaten.'

'I don't mind,' Barry said. 'As a matter of fact I don't remember a lot – about getting to the station and all. I felt awful – dazed and sick.'

But he remembered drawing up at the kerb at Waterloo. Before Mrs Padgitt could pay the driver a small car had swerved, stopped in front of their taxi with a screech of brakes, and Tim and Campers jumped out and ran back.

'They were trying to persuade her to go back to Campers' flat and talk it out. Saying it was the worst possible moment for her to take me to this school – "madness" Tim said it was – and that it might put me off, or something, for good. Mum kept on trying to take the suitcase out, and Tim pushed it back, and the driver got out and started shouting at Campers and Tim – it was a rare old rumpus. Then – well – I threw up. Just had time to get out – push my way out – but ...'

Andreas and Dimitri had begun to laugh. 'The blazer!' they cried, 'and the pants! The socks ... oh, oh ... Why did you not think to be sick in your cap?'

By now the entire Georgiou family was rocking, holding one another, tears streaming down their faces, till their mother cried, 'Stop! Hal and Barry will think we are all crazy!'

Hal didn't think them crazy but she did think their behaviour a bit rude. What with the queer foreign food and the wine that Mr Georgiou had poured into her glass, she was beginning to feel more than a little out of things. But when Barry laughed, 'It's a family joke,' seemingly quite at ease, she thought, well if he doesn't mind, why should I? Besides, they stopped as suddenly as they had begun.

'So of course you couldn't go to the college that day?' Dimitri prompted Barry.

They had gone, after all, to Campers' flat, for by then Mrs Padgitt, who had herself had a rough night, was too confused and tired to argue. Barry had been put to bed, the new school clothes removed by Tim to the nearest cleaner's, and while Barry slept, the grown-ups talked.

'I don't know what they said. But Tim must've taken Mum home to get some clean clothes for me to wear when I woke up. She took me back and didn't say any more about the new school that night.

'But I'll tell you something she did say,' Barry paused while Mrs Georgiou went into the house for more food, because he wanted her to hear what was coming. Hal sat back. Leaves tickled the back of her neck; an ear-wig fell on to her empty plate. Late sunlight freckled through the leaves; swallows darted near, catching insects in the still summer air. Though the front of Mr Georgiou's shop was on such a busy street, the back of the houses looked like cottages, like a scrap of the country left over in the middle of London, where there were small workshops and crazy chimney pots at all angles. Pipe smoke went up from a neighbouring garden where runner beans covered one wall.

'It wasn't true that Mum ever meant to marry Crimp's Dad,' Barry announced, while Mrs Georgiou dished out the next course. 'She used to meet him sometimes for a drink – they'd known each other once, but years ago. And he'd take her out to dinner sometimes. Smart places. Real lush. Oh – and once she did go to his house. But the rest of it – I don't know where Crimp got it from. She'd got him sized up all right Mum had. Crimp's dad, I mean.'

Barry looked round, wanting everyone to hear, but specially Mrs Georgiou. The fact that his mother had been in two minds about Mr Watson till recently, that she had freely admitted the attraction of his success – this he kept to himself.

Dimitri looked doubtful. 'And Cranmere College?'

'There wasn't any other reason that I can see except what she said. She wanted the best for me. And that old hen Mrs Roebuck had it all fixed.'

Hal poked at what was on her plate, a parcel of leaves covered in cheese sauce. Crimp, she thought, couldn't help telling whoppers, or worse, half-truths, half lies so you didn't know where you were with him. Funny thing was, Mary, who fancied herself so smart, had believed everything Crimp told her. Perhaps because Mary herself was a story-teller, Hal thought. They'd make up things together that they wanted to be true.

Mrs Georgiou sighed. 'It must be terrible to bring up a son without a father,' she reflected.

Hal, who hadn't been listening, decided that she wouldn't eat the leaves but that what was inside wasn't too bad. Harking back to what had recently been said, she put in, 'Crimp's dad never.'

'Never what?'

'Never wanted the best for his kid. Like you were saying.'

Mrs Georgiou answered, 'He is an evil man. At home we should have known what to do with him.'

'That is why people should live in villages or small towns,' said Mr Georgiou, 'small enough for everyone to know who are the wrongdoers. But in a big city they go unpunished.'

Hal felt some sympathy for the boys, who were showing similar signs of boredom and embarrassment to her own when her dad went on about Barbados.

Here they all were – she and Barry and the two younger Georgiou boys – all Londoners. Who wanted to go over all that stuff? Dimitri and Andreas hardly remembered their birthplace. To change the subject, she said, 'Crimp's run away.'

'Everyone knows that. He'll be back before long.'

'I don't think so. Nor Mary doesn't.'

Barry shook his head, 'He won't get far. Mr Watson was on to Mum after he'd been gone a day or two. Thought I might know something. As though I'd say if I did! He's set the police on him. And the Salvation Army.'

Andreas snorted, 'What's he want him back for – to beat him up?'

'I think he really might get away,' Hal persisted, 'he looks older than he is – and he's so strong. Mary had a card from him, from some port in the North. "Be seeing you," it said. And "Destroy this at once".'

'Maybe he meant it – he may come back when it's safe, and he's older. For Mary. And the kid. He fancied her.'

'He's a loner.' Dimitri's tone of voice expressed the baffled admiration and uncertainty they all felt about the unfathomable Crimp.

Mrs Georgiou brooded over the possible fate of the motherless boy so long that her husband had to remind her to fetch the coffee. As usual, their baby daughter had gone to sleep on her lap. Barry, being nearest, took her, naturally and comfortably, as he had often taken the sleeping Bell.

While they drank coffee, poured scalding out of a copper pot, and some smooth paste which tasted of peanuts and honey and other ingredients that Hal couldn't identify, Mrs Georgiou began speaking to Barry in a tone which suggested to Hal that something was coming up, something that needed saying but might not be welcome.

'I spoke with your mother. She has had a sad life – sad and hard. And all for you.'

Hal reflected how awful it might be living with your mum, on your own, with this sort of thing on your mind, not often able to forget it.

Barry was silent. 'Yeah,' he said after a bit, 'but she won't have it any more – a hard life, I mean.' He turned to Hal. 'She is going to get married. When she told me who it was I couldn't believe it.'

'Who?' Hal responded with interest.

'Mr Barnes at the Co-op – not where we live now, but where we used to live before I went into hospital.'

Hal's interest deflated.

'He was always on at her, it seems, but she wouldn't. He kept on writing. And once we met him again – one Sunday at my Auntie's. It was a surprise, I don't mind telling you, when she come out with it! He's a bit dull. But kind, all right. Pays her attention. Give her anything, he would. Give me this watch. We bin staying down there, where we lived before, but in his flat. And I can go back for holidays.'

'And you don't mind?' Mrs Georgiou asked. 'Your mother thought you might. But I told her nothing is worse than a boy without a father.'

'No.' He thought about it. 'No. I might've once. But now I'm glad. Won't have her on me mind.'

'Don't you know that it was because of you she never re-married? Jealous, she said you were. Anyone who came to the house or took her out . . .'

'A long time ago, p'raps. When I was a kid. But not now.'

'Not so long. But now you are beginning to grow up, and that is good. For you and for her.'

Hal shifted. The bench was beginning to cramp her thin

behind. This she only noticed because there'd been enough talk. About Barry's mum, and the Mr Barnes at the Co-op. Didn't seem to have much to do with the Barry she knew, and Jefferson, their life there. Maybe Barry wouldn't have to go home every holiday. There were these camps Tim had been talking about, places you could do anything you wanted like climbing or sailing.

Hal had seen something of Campers and Tim together. The first visit had been a painful one for her. But before long her sense of betrayal, and her obsession with Tim, began to seem childish and unreal, melting away in her affection for them both, and theirs for her. She and Campers had had a talk on their own, and Campers had explained that she had quarrelled with Tim because of his giving up his work at the Institute. 'Opting out,' she called it, money or no money. 'He didn't try hard enough,' she said. 'He's weak in a way.'

'You're right there,' Hal agreed, 'I told him so.'

It was like two grown-up women discussing a man they were both fond of.

Then Campers had said, 'We're going to re-decorate my flat. It'd be super if you could come and help. Next week-end?'

When the flat was finished, and the furniture put back, not without some half-laughing, half-serious disagreement and an appeal to Hal to decide for them, they sat back and ate supper in the lingering summer twilight. Hal, then, had had the strangest sense that, just by being there, she had somehow made things easier for them, coming together as they were, making a new start. Now, she shut her eyes and leant back against the wall, remembering the two of them standing in the doorway saying goodnight. 'Come again,'

Tim had said, 'we couldn't have managed without you. And there's still lots to do.'

There would be good times to share with them. The long summer holiday ahead, for instance. There was an idea they might take some of the people from the site off to one of these camps they'd spoken of. Barry could get a lot stronger. She began to make plans.

Barry, too, was looking ahead, though the vague thoughts that drifted through his mind, drowsily lulled by the sleeping child, were more like day-dreams, pictures, insubstantial as the smoke rings from Mr Georgiou's cigar. He would see his mother often, go home, sometimes, week-ends. And holidays. Might even ask his friends home. A whole floor at the top of Mr Barnes' shop was almost empty, used for storage. Christmas, now – that'd be the time! Plenty to eat – a vision of the shop, all lit up, stuffed with almonds and raisins, candied fruit, huge boxes of chocolates done up in ribbon.

Who would come? Hal, if only out of curiosity; he couldn't be sure she'd come for him – to be with him. He couldn't have put it into words, the sense that Hal liked to choose her own ground for battle or friendship.

Mary Malone, she'd come. For the food. And the comfort. His mum and Mr Barnes – Barry was confident he could bring them round if they were awkward about the baby. Unlikely though it seemed, Barry clung to the idea that Crimp would come back for her. And if he did – there'd be a place for him. For them both. Barry's world was warm and all-embracing, under the vine arbour.

'We really ought to be going,' Hal said. Her mum had got her Dad to be easier about her staying out, specially while the summer nights lasted. And if someone saw her right to her door. But not after dark.

No one moved. Barry, with the sleeping toddler in his arms, seemed miles away, looking up at the sky, a deepening blue through the leaves; his fair hair falling back, his fine-boned face sleepy, relaxed as she had sometimes remembered it since their night on the little hill under the ash saplings.

Turning away to see if she could get Dimitri to move, and so slide out along the bench, she caught Mr Georgiou's eye on her. He removed his cigar and inclined his head in a gesture that took account of both Barry and herself. It was the slightest, most delicate of movements; but it made Hal flush from her throat to the roots of her hair, the way she had at her first meeting with Barry.

Mrs Georgiou came back and took up the sleeping child. Barry got up, and murmuring their thanks, he and Hal slipped out through the kitchen and the side door.

Twenty-Four

On the way home they hardly spoke. With her hand held lightly in his, they moved swiftly, though half-sleepily, down familiar ways, past lit, closed shops, dark warehouses, people drinking outside pubs. Through an area waiting to be rebuilt, where lately houses had been, streets that were now corridors of iron, pasted with old, flapping bills, hiding dusty deserts, holding the day's heat like a slow oven.

A diesel engine hooted.

'Hurry!' Hal pulled at his hand.

They were beginning to wake up, to be aware of how late it was, how nearly dark.

As they climbed the stairs at the flats Hal said, 'Dad won't half carry on!'

'Nurts! Your mum told him you was growing up, didn't she? He'll have to let you come dancing soon. There's youth clubs, and that. Would you like to?'

'You know I can't dance.' Hal frowned, hating to be reminded of failure.

'Course you can. It's just a thing with you, not dancing. You run like a – like a cheetah.' It was true, her graceful, sinuous unconscious movement when running or walking. 'You just – I dunno – you don't let yourself go when you dance. Like Springy said. Time you learnt.'

The lift slid open. They stepped out into the high, cool

air and all at once Barry seized her hand. 'Move,' he cried, 'move!' (But his cry was a whisper lest they disturb the people in the flats.)

He twirled her round and left her, danced away from her, danced round her. 'Let go,' he whispered, 'dancing's how you feel. Let up!'

And somehow she was following him, they parted, came together, she was dancing her own dance, yet in answer to his, twisting, moving up the balcony, soundless except for the squeak of their sneakers on concrete. Before her turning eyes lights ran in rivers from far out in space as she twirled, then darkness, then light...

'That's enough!' The low voice, close to, startled Hal and she stopped dead in front of her own unlit doorway.

'Mum! How long've you been there?' Then, 'Hey – Barry!' she called softly. But Barry was away off up the wide balcony, beyond hearing, dancing for Hal, dancing for himself.

Hal came in and shut the door. 'That's just like him!'

'It'd have been nice to meet him,' her mother said, switching on the light in the kitchen and closing the door. 'Your dad's asleep – lucky for you!'

'I tell you, Mum, that's Barry all over. Doesn't know when to stop.'

'So it seems!' Mrs Piercy laughed happily, quietly, forgetting her own tiredness. As Hal turned to go to her own room she went on, 'Won't he wonder what's happened?'

'Let him!' Hal was as angry as she was breathless. Then, catching her mother's eye, she laughed, they both laughed for joy because of the dancing, smothering the sound in the sleeping flat.

In her bedroom Hal went to the window, crouched down

looking over the ceaseless life of the railway, brilliant under arc lights, freightliners, mail trains, passenger trains, slowing, speeding, gliding in and out and about one another. With her head still full of rhythm and movement it seemed to her that they, too, were moving in a pattern like dancers.

Hal sighed, her breath still coming fast. There was no foreseeing what Barry would do, how he would behave. Tomorrow he might lie in the Georgiou's garden, all energy spent. As though she didn't exist. Or he might turn up at the flat, yes, though he never had before – turn up and ring the bell, as though nothing had happened.

And she thought then, what *had* happened? She had danced – oh, how she had danced! Later, she remembered Mr Georgiou; how he had looked at them both. Everything that had been said before was hazy, though it had seemed important at the time.

Hal put her head down on the sill, ready for sleep. Her head was in such a muddle. She recalled her talk with her mother. How do you know if you fancy a feller? she had asked. For her mum there had been certainty – and when she hadn't been much older than Hal. For Hal there was none. But perhaps, after all, she was stuck with Barry. For the time being anyhow.

You could say, and it wasn't a bad feeling, they were stuck with each other.

Heard about the Puffin Club?

... it's a way of finding out more about Puffin books and authors, of winning prizes (in competitions), sharing jokes, a secret code, and perhaps seeing your name in print! When you join you get a copy of our magazine, *Puffin Post*, sent to you four times a year, a badge and a membership book. For details of subscription and an application form, send a stamped addressed envelope to:

The Puffin Club Dept A
Bath Road
Penguin Books Limited
Harmondsworth
Middlesex UB7 ODA

and if you live in Australia, please write to:

The Australian Puffin Club
Penguin Books Australia Limited
P.O. Box 257
Ringwood
Victoria 3134